# DEAD
# MAN'S
# CAT

# DEAD MAN'S CAT

## A Mystery

Carol Beach York

THOMAS NELSON INC.

Nashville • New York

No character in this story is intended to represent any actual person; all the incidents of the story are entirely fictional in nature.

*First edition*

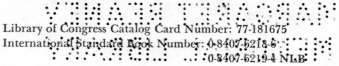
Library of Congress Catalog Card Number: 77-181675
International Standard Book Number: 0-8407-6218-6
0-8407-6219-4 NLB
Manufactured in the United States of America

ﺝ

With Love to Kathy
and her girls, Lori and Kelly

# Contents

PART ONE

# CALLING
# THE
# DEAD

## One:

# *Secrets of the Unknown*

Michael and Queenie first saw Mrs. Morley one gray autumn afternoon. They were sitting eating popsicles on the steps of the building where they lived in a third-floor apartment. Michael had nearly finished his popsicle and was watching with interest how long Queenie could make hers last. Michael had never known anyone who could make a popsicle last as long as his sister.

Michael was twelve, but Queenie was only ten years old. Her hair hung in her eyes and her two little bare knees, showing below the hem of her dress, were healing of a good skinning she had given them the day before trying to learn to ride Michael's bike. Her small tongue came out again and again, patiently licking the popsicle. She never took bites, the way Michael did; that's what made her popsicle last so long.

Her grayish-blue eyes were solemn, for it was a serious business to Queenie, eating popsicles. And occasionally she would hiccup.

It was because of her hiccups that their mother had given them the popsicles. "The last two we've got," Mrs. Allen had said, with the weariness of mothers whose kitchen cupboards never seem to have enough food.

11

It had rained earlier in the afternoon, and the side-walk was still damp. Puddles had formed in the paving of the street, reflecting in their small surfaces the cloud-cast sky above.

It was an old section of town, a shabby street, looking more bleak than usual in the aftermath of the rain.

Mrs. Morley came walking along carefully, avoiding the wettest spots. She was not very pleased with the look of Hopkins Street, for she did not like shabby places. She came along more and more hesitantly, thinking she should not have come at all.

But she had come this far, she thought to herself.

She compared addresses on the buildings with a slip of paper she held in one gloved hand.

Mrs. Morley was no longer young. Her girlish prettiness had given way to gray hair and a double chin and a plump-ness around her middle, below which her two rather spindly legs gave her a birdlike appearance. She was neatly dressed, but not in her best, of course. Her errand was not of the best-clothes kind, like Sunday mornings at church or Friday afternoons at her ladies' club luncheons. But she did have her gloves, and a small blue hat, and a handbag that was really almost good enough for best. Two gold initials were clipped on the side of the handbag: A.M., which stood for Amanda Morley and not the time of day, as she was so often teased about.

Securely under one arm was tucked a large, square, flat package in a brown paper bag.

What am I doing on this dismal street? she thought to herself; and the two children sitting on the steps of the building which she suddenly realized was the address she was looking for did not brighten her outlook. She stood on the pavement frowning at the old apartment building, its red brick weathered and faded, its front steps in need of a good coat of paint. Mrs. Morley had come to consult a medium in the hopes of contacting her dead husband, and it occurred to her with a sense of frustration that this medium could not be very good or she would have moved on to better quarters.

But she had come this far. It seemed better to go on than to turn back.

Mrs. Morley went past the children—noting that the little girl was dripping popsicle on her dress—and stepped into the entryway of the building.

The entry looked better than she had expected, judging from the outside appearance of the building; but almost at once she met a fresh disappointment. The names on several of the mailboxes had been worn beyond reading, and among the names she could make out there was not the one she was looking for.

She opened the entry door and went out again, standing at the top of the steps and staring down at the children sitting below.

"Does a Mrs. Poldini live in this building?" Mrs. Morley said to the backs of their heads.

The little girl turned and stared up over the top of her dripping popsicle. The boy stood up. "Second floor. 2-D."

"Thank you," Mrs. Morley replied, and disappeared back into the entry again.

"I told you I recognized her," Michael said to Queenie with satisfaction. But he didn't expect Mrs. Morley to remember him. Yesterday when he had handed her Mrs. Poldini's handbill, Mrs. Morley had not even glanced at him. She had her head bent against the wind, and he had thrust the handbill into her hand as she hurried by.

Michael sat down on the steps again and returned his

attention to a tall, heavy-set man he had been watching. The man had come along the street some distance behind Mrs. Morley. Something in his attitude had caught Michael's attention, and now he noticed that the man had come to a stop across the street, almost directly opposite Michael and Queenie's building. He had stopped and stood looking at the doorway where Mrs. Morley had entered. He did not move on.

Michael wondered if the man had been following Mrs. Morley and was waiting for her to come out.

Mrs. Morley made her way up the apartment's inner stairway to the second floor. She hesitated at the top of the steps, her hand on the railing. The hallway ahead was deserted. The first doorway at the head of the stairs had a metal plate: 2-A. From somewhere on the floor above, a baby was crying fretfully.

Mrs. Morley began to go along the hallway.

There were two doors on each side, and the rear door on the right was marked 2-D. There was also a small white card stuck into the door frame with a thumbtack: MRS. POLDINI.

Mrs. Morley hesitated again before this door. The paper slip, the handbill Michael had thrust into her hand on a street corner the day before, crinkled softly as she moved it in her fingers . . . deciding . . . still deciding whether it was the right thing that she had come.

## CALL BACK THE DEAD

*Speak to your loved ones who have gone beyond*
*Receive messages from them*

*Mrs. Poldini can reveal to you the secrets of the unknown*
*712 Hopkins Street*

Mrs. Morley shifted her parcel to a more secure position under her arm and lifted a gloved finger to the doorbell. She had come this far, and her need was so great. Nearly twenty-five thousand dollars might depend upon Mrs. Poldini's help. And Mrs. Morley had, for the moment, nowhere else to turn for help.

She pressed the bell, waited, and was about to ring again when the door opened abruptly and she found herself face to face with a large stoop-shouldered old woman wearing a brilliant red fringed shawl and a dark-blue turban. From the edges of the turban, tendrils of gray hair had been drawn free to form a row of flat curls across the broad forehead. The woman's skin was swarthy, her eyes large and dark. She was peering so intently out of the doorway that Mrs. Morley felt as though the woman had reached out and touched her.

"Mrs. Poldini?"

"Ye-es."

The voice was surprisingly soft, considering the rather violent impression made by the red-fringed shawl and great peering eyes.

"I—I—" Mrs. Morley hesitated and tightened her grip on the parcel. "I have one of your advertisements . . ." She held out the handbill almost apologetically.

The woman stood back from the door.

"Come in."

As Mrs. Morley stepped in—not without some misgivings—the old woman closed the door. She stood for a moment looking at Mrs. Morley.

"You come to learn the secrets of the unknown?"

There was a foreign sound to the way she pronounced her words, and she reminded Mrs. Morley of nothing so much as an ancient gypsy woman astray from some far off mid-European caravan.

"I wish to contact my dead husband."

The dark eyes glowed below the turban, the fringe swayed gently on the edges of the shawl.

I should not have come, Mrs. Morley thought for the hundredth time; but by now she was in apartment 2-D and the door was closed behind her.

"All will be revealed," the woman said. She nodded her large head slowly. The great eyes closed for a moment, as though even then she was consulting the unknown, the place beyond, and all the mysteries of the universe.

Opening her eyes to the present moment, to the known and revealed, and the very material universe, Mrs. Poldini gestured to a chair.

"Sit. A moment only and I am with you."

She disappeared through a doorway, and Mrs. Morley was left alone in one of the strangest rooms she had ever seen. Several ancient, faded green velour chairs stood along the walls like sentinels. By the windows was a small round table with a long purple cloth draped to the floor. A worn Persian rug too large for the room had been rolled under at the edges, so that Mrs. Morley had the sensation that the floor was curving upward at the sides.

A dilapidated piano stood against one wall, and an empty bird cage hung from a stand by the doorway to the kitchen.

Something seemed to be cooking in the kitchen. A warm, steamy vapor filled the rooms. For a moment Mrs. Morley thought she could not breathe—and surely she could not sit on one of those soiled green chairs.

Mrs. Poldini reappeared. She had put several gold bracelets on her flabby arms and hooked a pair of dangling gold earrings into her long ears.

Rearranging her shawl, she crossed the room to the purple table. She sat down beside it and, turning her eyes upon Mrs. Morley yet one more time, announced:

"We begin."

## Two:

# Dead Man

If Mrs. Morley felt doubtful about what she could see of Mrs. Poldini's living room, she would have been even more disturbed to see the rest of the apartment.

Besides the living room, where Mrs. Poldini conducted her "business" at the round purple-covered table, there were the kitchen and a small bedroom. The kitchen, as Mrs. Morley had noted, was the room from which the steamy vapor floated out to the other rooms.

It was Mrs. Poldini's belief that it was unhealthy to live in a dry atmosphere, and if she was not making chicken stew or boiling cabbage—which served to moisten the air—she kept her teakettle on a simmer, removing the lid so it did not whistle. Mrs. Poldini drank large amounts of tea, and it was handy to have hot water always ready in the kettle, as well as having the air humidified.

None of Mrs. Poldini's dishes matched; none of the little row of plants on her kitchen windowsill looked well, despite the moist atmosphere with which they were blessed.

The bedroom was small and dark, with only one tiny north-facing window. It was cluttered with clothes, even with the old spangled dresses that Mrs. Poldini had worn years before, when she was with the circus. She had saved them all. She also saved shoes, and in this small bedroom she had managed to cram some forty-odd pairs. Some had been saved from circus days and others bought at rummage sales and secondhand stores in the neighborhood. When Michael and Queenie visited Mrs. Poldini, Queenie was often allowed to try on the shoes and hobble around on the too-big Persian rug or click across on the worn kitchen linoleum while the teakettle hissed and the empty bird cage rocked gently on its hook.

It was just as well that Mrs. Morley was confined to only the main room; it contained all the oddness she was able to stand for the moment—and she would no doubt have turned and fled had she not had that twenty-five thousand dollars so firmly and longingly in her mind.

"When I was child, my grandfather come to window of my room and talk to me," Mrs. Poldini began with a heavy, mournful air.

Mrs. Morley tried to look politely interested. But what had Mrs. Poldini's grandfather to do with anything?

She soon found out.

"He was gone beyond for five years."

"Gone beyond?" Mrs. Morley echoed uncertainly.

"Gone beyond."

Mrs. Morley realized suddenly that Mrs. Poldini meant that her grandfather had been dead.

"I see," Mrs. Morley said faintly.

"He call me to window. He have message for my father to go to another city to live. Life would be good there."

Mrs. Poldini paused and shrugged sadly. "This is all of message. My mother come into room and my grandfather is not there anymore. He never come again."

"Oh."

"But from others who have gone beyond I receive the messages for loved ones. So it will be with you."

"Yes . . . well . . ." Mrs. Morley shifted her parcel uneasily. It seemed she was going to have to sit on one of the ancient green chairs after all. Mrs. Poldini was motioning to one opposite her own at the purple table.

"Sit, and we begin."

Gingerly Mrs. Morley perched on the edge of the chair. She held the parcel on her lap.

"Your name?"

"Mrs. Morley."

"Mrs. Mor-ley." The great dark eyes closed, a thickly-veined old hand passed across Mrs. Poldini's forehead. "Yes—Yes—I feel the vibrations. They come."

Mrs. Morley leaned slightly forward in the chair.

The great dark eyes remained closed; the great turbaned head swayed slightly.

"The vibrations are good . . . the unknown is revealed to us . . . all can be revealed."

Mrs. Morley certainly hoped so. Her hands clenched with determination. Twenty-five thousand dollars was at stake. George had been dead only a week—oh, if only he had not yet gotten so far "beyond" that she could not reach him.

Fleetingly, Mrs. Morley released her doubts about Mrs. Poldini. The fact that she lived in such a poor neighborhood need not necessarily mean anything. The woman looked eccentric enough to have a mattress stuffed with

money. That was probably it, Mrs. Morley thought, a
mattress stuffed with money.

In the midst of these considerations, Mrs. Morley was
unprepared for the opening of the great dark eyes. Without warning, they were piercingly upon her again, as
though Mrs. Poldini were waiting for something, some
sign, perhaps, of Mrs. Morley's faith.

Mrs. Morley cleared her throat delicately. "I—I have
heard that when you wish to contact the . . . the departed"
—Mrs. Morley hesitated over the word—"I have heard
that sometimes it is helpful to have something of theirs,
of the . . . the departed."

Mrs. Poldini answered with a grave nod of her head.
The gold earrings swung.

Mrs. Morley placed her paper parcel on the table and
opened it with unsteady fingers. She reached in and drew
out a large framed photograph of her late husband,
George Morley, shoe salesman. He had always complained
of poor health, until nobody listened to him any longer;
and even when his last illness took such a bad turn, nobody really expected him to die. And, dying, to leave
such an exasperating puzzle behind.

From the frame her husband's face stared blandly up
at Mrs. Morley, as he had so often stared at her in life.

Mrs. Morley offered the photograph to Mrs. Poldini,
who placed it upon the table squarely before her and
studied it thoughtfully. She moved it a few inches, so that
the light did not reflect on the glass covering the photograph, and then she studied it again silently for several
minutes. The photograph was about twelve by fifteen
inches, in a plain gold frame. The face of George Morley
was ordinary, a middle-aged man with a large nose and

puffy cheeks. But it was not without redeeming qualities. His eyes were kindly, and his hair had not begun to recede. If he had lived to be ninety he would probably still have had a good head of hair.

Sometimes there were a great many things Mrs. Poldini could tell from photographs, but aside from the facts that George Morley had been neat, overweight, probably kind, and not going bald, there was not much to see in this photograph.

Mrs. Morley waited expectantly. She did not dare to disturb Mrs. Poldini, who sat so motionlessly contemplating the photograph that Mrs. Morley thought perhaps she had already gone into a trance of some kind.

Mrs. Morley could hear the baby upstairs begin to cry again. And she could hear a radio playing, but she could not tell whether it was in the same apartment with the crying baby or not.

At last Mrs. Poldini sat back in her chair, crossed her hands in her lap, and said,

"I think now you tell me about husband and why we must call him from the beyond."

## Three:

# Dead Man's Will

"My husband was not a rich man," Mrs. Morley began slowly. "We lived a simple life. We have a car and a small house, paid for, and our daughter is married and has a nice home of her own. We weren't really needy in any way, but we did not have a great deal of money saved. We *could* have had." Mrs. Morley could not help the note of vexation; George had been so unreasonable, it seemed.

"We *could* have had money saved, but every time he got a few extra dollars, my husband would buy stamps. I always said *I* would rather have the money in the bank, safe and sound and paying interest. But George always said his stamp collection was a better investment, better than interest from a bank.

"Well"—Mrs. Morley drew herself up straighter in the chair with a self-righteous sigh—"I don't know if he was right about that part or not. I suppose some of his stamps did increase in value, but of course I can't be sure; I don't really know anything about stamps. But he was set in his mind about it, and there wasn't anything I could do. The last time he had the collection appraised, it was supposed to be worth nearly twenty-five thousand dollars."

A shadow flickered across the depths of the great dark eyes below the turban. Mrs. Poldini did not have a mattress stuffed with money, as Mrs. Morley suspected; in fact, at the moment, Mrs. Poldini's funds were very low. Twenty-five thousand dollars sounded like a million to her.

"To make a long story short"—Mrs. Morley's voice took on a grieved tone—"George made up a will just a few days before he died. He didn't mention anything else in the will, just the stamp collection. He said he bequeathed it to whoever finds it—'my wife, my daughter, my brother—or anyone else it may be.' Those are the exact words of the will: 'my wife, my daughter, my brother—or anyone else it may be.' "

Mrs. Morley paused to let this sink in.

Mrs. Poldini said, "Life is strange."

Mrs. Morley picked at the gold initials on her handbag.

"Naturally we've looked everywhere in the house," she continued gloomily. "My daughter Dorothea has come over from her house to help me. She doesn't want the stamps for herself, but she doesn't want Arthur to find them, or anyone else, of course. Dorothea agrees with me that the stamps should by all rights be mine.

"And Arthur and his wife come over and hunt around —I don't know who's worse, Arthur or Letitia. They're so *greedy*. My husband never got along with his brother very well. I can't imagine why he would even mention him in the will. Now Arthur feels that gives him the right to come over whenever he chooses and paw around my house—everything's topsy-turvy, and we still can't find the stamps."

Mrs. Poldini's eyelids were slowly drooping, as if her thoughts were too heavy upon her mind to bear.

"I've been frantic, of course, because the stamps should be mine, not Arthur's. It was money I could have used for things for the house and things for Dorothea when she was growing up. But George was always buying those stamps. Now at least I should have them and be able to sell them. They don't belong to Arthur or anybody else who finds them! It was just cruel of George to make such a will."

Mrs. Poldini's eyelids grew more droopy. The man in the photograph did not look cruel.

"I have looked *every*place I can think of," Mrs. Morley said, "and then the other day on the street somebody handed me your advertisement, and at first I didn't think much about it, just stuffed it in my handbag to throw out when I came to a trash bin—but I forgot, and this morning when I was looking for something else in the handbag, there it was. I got to thinking that perhaps that was the answer. I could contact George and ask him where the stamps are, and remind him that his first duty is to me, his wife. Don't you think that is his first duty, Mrs. Poldini? Twenty-five thousand dollars is nothing to play games with."

Mrs. Poldini agreed; twenty-five thousand dollars was nothing to play games with at all.

But the man in the photograph had not looked mischievous. Not the kind of man who would play games with twenty-five thousand dollars. And he had not looked cruel.

There must be some other explanation.

# Four:

## *The Follower*

Mrs. Poldini drew the curtains at her windows. The room took on an eerie shadowiness that made prickles run up and down Mrs. Morley's back under her not-quite-best clothes. She could see the gold initials on her handbag in the dimness, and they gave her what small sense she had of clinging to the real, everyday world.

"Place hands on photograph," Mrs. Poldini directed.

She had already placed her hands, palms down, on the part of the photograph nearest her, and Mrs. Morley did the same. Their fingertips touched.

"We think of husband's name," Mrs. Poldini said. She rolled her eyes to the ceiling, fastened them there, and spoke no more.

The silence was broken by the fretting baby in the apartment above, but after a while Mrs. Morley didn't hear the crying anymore, she was concentrating so hard on the name George Morley. George Morley. George Morley. She held the words in her mind like a hand gripping a rock.

The baby stopped, and the silence deepened. The shadows deepened. Mrs. Poldini was as motionless as a statue. Finally Mrs. Morley realized she had been sitting so stiffly and tensely that she was almost forgetting to breathe.

*George Morley,* she thought—and she tried to rid her mind of resentment for what he had done. He probably wouldn't want to be contacted from the beyond if he thought she was mad at him. But it was hard to forgive all the differences they had had over the years—arguments over his buying stamps, arguments over his smelly pipes, his baseball games on television, his cats—and in years farther back there had been arguments about Dorothea. Dorothea's new party dresses, Dorothea's dancing lessons, and once a house that Dorothea had wanted to move to, a big house, much nicer than the little house they had.

"There's never enough money for anything *nice,*" Dorothea had wailed. She was thirteen then, and she wanted to live in that big, beautiful house.

It was hard for Mrs. Morley to forget these things. But she tried.

"George Morley," she said to herself over and over. "Come and tell me where you put that stamp album—please, George."

After a long time Mrs. Poldini opened her eyes.

"He not come to us today."

"Oh." Mrs. Morley's disappointment was complete. It was just like George, she couldn't help feeling. And then she said, "It's just like him not to come; he always was unreasonable."

"The dead not speak unless we call with love," Mrs. Poldini said in a tone of mournful reproach.

"George knows I love him," Mrs. Morley protested.

"Why else would I have put up with him all those years?"

Mrs. Poldini thought about this with a melancholy air.

"We be patient," she said at last. "We clear minds. Each time we come a step closer."

Mrs. Morley sank back in the green chair. Her whole body ached from sitting upright and holding her hands so rigidly on the photograph.

"Perhaps tomorrow he speak to us," Mrs. Poldini said. "We have begun, we continue. Be patient."

After a moment she rose and opened the curtains. It had grown quite dusky outside and the dim late-afternoon light did not brighten the room much. Mrs. Poldini turned on a lamp by the table, springing into clearer view again suddenly with her row of curls on her forehead and her red fringe fluttering. Her bracelets jangled softly as she moved.

Mrs. Morley smoothed her skirt and stood up. She was not sure if she would return or not. It was just *like* George to be stubborn, even in the beyond. Her time might be better spent at home looking for the stamps in a more practical way. She certainly didn't want Arthur and that fat Letitia finding them first. Mrs. Morley had her old age to think of and the twenty-five thousand dollars would help a lot.

"Leave photograph with me," Mrs. Poldini directed, swaying in the lamplight. Her dark eyes were even now upon the face of George Morley lying on the tabletop.

Mrs. Morley hesitated. Keeping the photograph was just a trick of Mrs. Poldini's to be sure she would return.

But after a moment she said, "I guess that would be all right." Her eyes touched the photograph briefly, and

she looked away. She found it very wearing upon her
nerves to contemplate that bland, smiling face. She
opened her handbag and took out her wallet.

"How much do I owe you?"

Mrs. Poldini lifted a hand in faint protest. Her bracelets slid along her arm, shining in the lamplight.

"It is not necessary now. When we reach the beyond."

Mrs. Morley hesitated. It was tempting just to stick her
wallet back in her handbag and leave. But on the other
hand, she might not ever come back to contact the beyond,
and she felt she owed Mrs. Poldini at least a few dollars
for her time already spent.

Mrs. Morley opened her wallet. "Let me give you
something now anyway," she said, "on account."

Mrs. Poldini's tranquil gaze was fastened upon the bills
she could see in the wallet.

"If you wish."

Mrs. Morley extracted a five-dollar bill from the wallet.
She paid her way where she went, never ran up debts
or tried to get something for nothing. During all her
years of marriage she had been frugal, never bought more
than the budget could afford. George had never really
appreciated what a good, thrifty wife she had been.
Lot of good it had done her, though. Leaving his stamp
album to whoever found it indeed!

Mrs. Morley went out into the darkening afternoon.
A fine rain had begun to fall again, and she walked
quickly along the street. It was four blocks to her house,
and she wanted to get there before the rain began to fall
more heavily and ruined her blue hat. That she had

come out on such an afternoon without an umbrella was proof of the distracted state of her thoughts these last days since she had read that will.

She did not notice Michael and Queenie, who had moved from the steps and were around the corner at the side of the building. Unmindful of the rain, they were taking turns throwing a ball against the wall. Nor did Mrs. Morley notice the man across the street who had been standing in a doorway and now came down the street and followed Mrs. Morley.

But Michael and Queenie saw the man. They stopped playing with the ball and watched as he walked at some distance behind Mrs. Morley.

At the corner Mrs. Morley turned, and the children watched until the man reached the corner and turned too and they could not see him any longer.

# Five

# The Lost Wallet

Another proof of Mrs. Morley's distracted state of mind was that she had forgotten to replace her wallet in her handbag. She had left it lying on the edge of the purple-covered table; and she had not been gone many minutes before Mrs. Poldini, approaching the table with the intention of studying the photograph further, spied the wallet lying beside the gold frame. But it was too late then to catch Mrs. Morley.

Just as well, Mrs. Poldini thought to herself. There might be something she could learn from the wallet. She sat down at the table and opened the wallet with interest.

There was twenty-two dollars and forty-six cents in the two money compartments. Besides that, there was a dry cleaner's claim check, an identification card giving Mrs. Morley's name and address, and a dentist's card with the notation of Mrs. Morley's next appointment. There were also several snapshots of a girl with yellow hair, which seemed to be the same girl at different ages. The daughter Dorothea Mrs. Morley had mentioned, Mrs. Poldini decided.

It was a neat, tidy, ordinary wallet, and it did not tell Mrs. Poldini much except that Mrs. Morley took care of

31

her teeth and was a fortunate woman to have twenty-two dollars and forty-six cents—plus the five-dollar bill she had given Mrs. Poldini.

Mrs. Poldini considered the outside of the wallet. It was a dark-brown pin seal with a gold clasp on the change compartment. And it was nearly new.

By and by Mrs. Poldini put the wallet in her dress pocket, where its bulge was concealed by the overlapping of the red fringe on her shawl. Then she went into her steamy kitchen to look at the chicken stew she was preparing for her supper.

She was just getting a spoon to stir the stew when Michael and Queenie came rushing upstairs and rang her doorbell. They wanted to tell her about the man following Mrs. Morley, and they wanted to hear about Mrs. Morley herself. Mrs. Poldini often discussed her visitors with them, and they were sure she would tell them all about Mrs. Morley.

They followed Mrs. Poldini back into the kitchen and sniffed hungrily. The stew simmered on the stove. Bits of onion and carrot floated on the top of the yellowish liquid bubbling gently in a pot with a broken handle.

"You are hungry, I suppose," Mrs. Poldini said to them gloomily.

She set out two of her unmatching bowls. Queenie sat right down at the kitchen table and looked expectantly at the stewpot from beneath her straggling hair.

When the stew was ladled into the bowls, Queenie picked out all the pieces of onion as she ate and pushed them aside. She was always afraid that one of those soft white pieces might get on her spoon by mistake—and worse, get into her mouth and down her throat. She could not stand the thought of that slimy white thing in her throat.

"Eat your onions," Mrs. Poldini said.

Queenie looked up from under her hair and smiled disarmingly.

Mrs. Poldini poured herself a cup of tea and settled down heavily into one of her creaky kitchen chairs. Watching Queenie separate her onions from the rest of the stew, Mrs. Poldini told them about Mrs. Morley and her dead husband and the missing stamp collection.

"Gee, twenty-five thousand dollars!" Michael whistled between his teeth. "Did you contact him?"

"Not today. Only with patience we call back the dead."

Mrs. Poldini closed her great eyes and retired into the dark place behind. The children stared at her admiringly.

"Boy, I bet she's pretty mad not to be able to find those stamps," Michael said wisely.

Mrs. Poldini did not open her eyes at once, but then slowly the lids slid back, revealing the glowing darkness of her eyes. She reached into her dress pocket and took out the wallet.

"Hey—is that hers? What'd you do, rob her?" Michael's eyes grew wide with excitement.

"I rob no one," Mrs. Poldini said. "She forget. She think only of stamps."

"Let's see what's inside," Michael suggested eagerly.

Mrs. Poldini appeared to hesitate. She smoothed the soft pin seal under her broad fingertips.

"Aw, come on," Michael urged. "Gee, there's isn't any harm in just looking, is there? Maybe it's got her address somewhere, and I could return it to her and get a big reward."

Queenie lapped up the last of her stew, pushed aside the bowl, and rested her arms on the table. She put her chin on her arms, so that she was just eye level with Mrs. Poldini's hands and the pin-seal wallet.

"I guess no harm to look," Mrs. Poldini admitted.

Michael and Queenie watched while she opened the wallet. There were the pictures of the girl with yellow hair. There was the twenty-two dollars and forty-six cents. There were the cleaner's ticket, the identification card, and Mrs. Morley's dental arrangements.

"Look at all that green stuff," Michael exclaimed when he saw the money. There were three fives and seven singles, and it made a fat bunch all together like that in the narrow back section of the wallet.

Mrs. Poldini laid Mrs. Morley's money out on the table, and they all looked at it thoughtfully. Each one of them could certainly have used that money. Queenie laid her head over on the side, her cheek pressing against her thin arm. She could feel her own breath on her hand.

"Gee, I sure wish that was *mine,*" Michael said.

Mrs. Poldini looked at the money with a grieved expression that it was not hers—or, second best, Michael's— but belonged instead to a woman who would no doubt sooner or later be the possessor of twenty-five thousand dollars. Life was unfair. Mrs. Morley did not need this skimpy little twenty-two dollars and forty-six cents.

But at last Mrs. Poldini gathered the bills together and squeezed them into the back of the wallet. She took out the identification card with Mrs. Morley's address and passed it across the table to Michael.

"Maybe you get reward," she said, "maybe not."

"Gee, she ought to give me *some*thing if I return it."

Michael was indignant at the thought that such an act could go unrewarded.

Mrs. Poldini stirred her tea. "We wait and see," she said. She handed the wallet to Michael.

"After school tomorrow you take to her. Maybe you get reward, maybe not."

Queenie swept back her hair and carried her bowl to the sink. She would have liked to stay awhile and try on some of Mrs. Poldini's shoes, but it was late. It was suppertime, and their mother would be looking for them.

She carefully rinsed out the bowl and poked the left-over pieces of onion down the drain.

The apartment where Mrs. Morley had heard the baby crying was Michael and Queenie's apartment. It was directly upstairs from Mrs. Poldini's, and the children's mother often complained that she could smell Mrs. Poldini cooking cabbage.

The fretting baby was Michael and Queenie's little sister. She had been fretful for several days now, and Mrs. Allen had been up with her several nights. This particular afternoon the baby had fussed more than ever, and Mrs. Allen was late getting supper. She did not scold Michael and Queenie for coming in late, although she gave them a suspicious look. She didn't approve of their friendship with Mrs. Poldini, but it was hard for her to keep track of them every minute, especially with the baby to look after.

"I suppose you've been down at that Mrs. Poldini's spoiling your appetites," she said as she set out their supper.

"I'm starved," Michael answered, which did not com-

mit him one way or the other of having visited Mrs.
Poldini. He considered telling his mother about the
wallet, but thought better of it. He would surprise her
when he had the reward.

Mrs. Allen's attention was diverted from Michael and
Queenie almost at once anyway, because the baby began
to cry again. Mrs. Allen had thought the baby was asleep
at last, and lines of weariness and strain showed around
her eyes. There was her mending undone on a chair by
the window, and in the kitchen the laundry was still in
the laundry basket waiting to be sorted and put away.
Her work was never done.

"You two might as well eat now," she said. "Your
father won't be home for a while."

Mr. Allen worked in a garage nearby, and on busy
days he was often late getting home in the evenings.
He came in when the children were halfway through
their supper. Queenie was picking the crust off her
bread.

"Crust makes your hair curly," he said to her, tousling
the top of her forlorn head as he sat down at the table.

Queenie smiled at him complacently.

"Queenie, eat your bread right," Mrs. Allen said.

"If we had a dog, he could have all Queenie's crusts,"
Michael said, for about the sixty millionth time.

"Never mind dogs," his mother said sternly.

"They aren't any trouble at all—" Michael began, but
his father's foot nudged him under the table. It was not
the time to bother his mother about a dog. But then
sometimes Michael thought there never was a right time.
He would grow up and be an old man and never have

a dog. Unless, of course, he grew up and moved away and then he would have six dogs all at once if he wanted.

He went to bed that night with Mrs. Morley's wallet under his pillow in case of a burglary. He felt very important with all that money so close.

PART TWO

# DEAD
# MAN'S
# CAT

## Six:

# *Returning the Wallet*

The next day after school Michael and Queenie went to return Mrs. Morley's wallet. They found her house without any difficulty, a two-story brown frame house on Linden Street. The yard needed a good raking; Mrs. Morley, having been lately occupied with hunting for the stamp album, had allowed other duties to slip.

In the yard next door, a boy's bike was propped against a tree. It was just the kind of bike Michael would like to have, if he could have a new bike. Only the other day, when Queenie was trying to ride, a pedal had fallen off Michael's bike, and the chain was always slipping, and the seat was worn and wobbly. A multitude of problems engulfed Michael when he thought about his bike.

Linden Street was a pleasant street of small houses, the kind of street where there would be flower beds in summertime and people mowing their lawns in the sunshine.

But now it was nearing winter. No one was out mowing lawns.

A laundry truck was making a delivery across the street, and a high wind tossed leaves along in the gutter by the curbing.

The children went up the walk to the front-porch steps. Mrs. Morley's house was plainly marked by an address plate on the wall by her door: 114. There was no doubt it was the right house.

Michael had the wallet in his pocket. All through the day at school he had kept reaching in to feel that the wallet was still there safe and sound. Twenty-two dollars and forty-six cents was worth keeping a good watch over.

"I don't like this place," Queenie announced as they stood at the bottom of the porch steps.

"For Pete's sake." Michael breathed out the words with exasperation. Just like a girl, he thought.

"It's queer-looking," she said. And indeed the house did have an unwelcoming air about it, heightened by the accumulation of dead, wet leaves across the yard and walk.

But Michael went boldly up the steps to the porch, and Queenie trailed meekly behind.

The door was opened by the man they had seen following Mrs. Morley.

He seemed to loom suddenly above them before they had much more than rung the bell. He wore the same dark coat, but no hat. His eyes were overhung by dark brows, and he was frowning at them. There was no mistaking it was the same man.

Before Michael could say anything, the man asked abruptly:

"What do you kids want?"

Michael felt they had interrupted him in something.

"Is Mrs. Morley home?"

"No, she's not here. What do you want with her?"

As he spoke, an expression of recognition and then suspicion crossed the man's face. Weren't these the same two kids who had been sitting on the steps of the building where Mrs. Morley had gone the day before?

"When will she be back?" Michael asked. He could feel Queenie pressing closer to him, seeking protection from the tall, cross man.

"I don't know." The man's frown of suspicion deepened. "She's out shopping."

A noise behind made the man turn and take a step back, right on the tail of a scrawny, half-grown yellow cat which flew out past his legs with a dreadful screech. As they watched, the cat shot down the porch steps and across the yard, disappearing from sight under a row of bushes.

". . . fool cat . . ." the man muttered under his breath. "Get out and stay out. Good riddance."

Michael backed a step or two away from the door. He almost knocked Queenie over, she was standing so close behind him.

"Hey, now, what do you kids want to see Mrs. Morley about?"

The man seemed on the verge of coming out of the house after them, and Michael instinctively knew he could not trust this man—and he didn't want to give him Mrs. Morley's wallet and all that money.

"Nothing important," Michael mumbled, wishing Queenie would stop getting in his way so he could get to the stairs.

The man glowered at them from the doorway. Michael was sure he could see right through the material of his trousers to where the wallet lay in his pocket. At that moment the wallet weighed about a ton.

Michael kept backing away, nudging Queenie along.

"What's the matter with you kids?" The man leaned toward them accusingly.

"We'll come back later," Michael said.

This time he took Queenie's hand and pulled her along down the porch steps. The man came out on the porch and stood watching as they hurried down the walk to the street. The yellow cat came out from under a bush and Queenie tried to pet it, but it hissed at her and drew back into the bushes, its glowing green eyes watching them from the shelter of the branches.

"Nice kitty, nice kitty," Queenie called to the cat. But the cat would not come out from the bushes.

"Come on, will you?" Michael urged Queenie. He could see the man standing on the porch watching them, and he wanted to get away from him. He thought any moment the man might come down the steps after them. He looked mean like that.

Michael dragged Queenie along the street as she kept looking back at the cat. When they reached the corner Michael was glad to see the man had gone back inside the house.

Now that he was away from the man, Michael was not so sure what to do next. He didn't want the burden of that wallet and money through another night and another day at school. He didn't want to go back and give it to the man.

They stood indecisively at the corner a few minutes, and then, as chance would have it, Mrs. Morley herself appeared coming along toward her house.

"Hey, Queenie, here she comes now," Michael said with relief. And forgetting that Mrs. Morley was still almost a stranger to them, they began to run along the street to meet her.

When Mrs. Morley saw the two children running along the street toward her she did not dream that they were coming to meet *her*—or that they would know her name.

"Mrs. Morley . . ."

Michael came to a breathless stop in front of Mrs. Morley, Queenie close behind. Her hair fell in her face, and she was beginning to hiccup.

"You left your wallet at Mrs. Poldini's—and we brought it back," Michael burst out eagerly. He pulled the wallet from his pocket and thrust it at the surprised Mrs. Morley.

Only a few minutes before, in the grocery store, Mrs. Morley had realized that her wallet was not in her purse. She was returning home to look for it, annoyed that she had not been able to do her shopping.

"My wallet! Oh, I'm so glad you found it!"

Mrs. Morley took the wallet from Michael's hands, which did not look too clean, and she could not resist the impulse to brush her glove over the surface.

Looking more closely now, she thought she did remember these children. They had been sitting on the front steps of Mrs. Poldini's building. This was the boy who had told her Mrs. Poldini lived on the second floor.

"She found it after you left," Michael said. "We're friends of hers and she said we could bring it back to you today after school."

"Well, thank you very much."

Mrs. Morley could not resist another temptation. She snapped open the wallet and began to look through it.

"Everything's there," Michael spoke up hastily. "All your money and stuff."

Mrs. Morley looked embarrassed.

"I'm sure it is. I was just looking."

Then there did not seem to be anything else to say for the moment. Mrs. Morley looked at the children and the children looked at her. Michael was hoping Mrs. Morley was deciding how big a reward she would give them.

What Mrs. Morley finally said was:

"There's an ice-cream store down in the next block. Wouldn't you like to have some ice cream? You ought to have something for your trouble."

Michael groaned inwardly with disappointment. He had hoped for a couple of dollars, or maybe even one of the five-dollar bills. Not ice cream. But something was better than nothing. He glanced at Queenie, who was nodding her head agreeably between hiccups.

"Queenie gets hiccups all the time," he said to Mrs. Morley, who was regarding Queenie with curiosity.

Queenie hiccuped loudly.

"Come along," Mrs. Morley said with more enthusiasm. "My little girl Dorothea used to get hiccups sometimes, and ice cream always stopped them. It's the coldness."

Mrs. Morley put her wallet into her handbag and led the way along the street toward the ice-cream parlor. It was a small place with round tables and spindly white iron chairs. There were also booths along one wall, and Michael said, "Hey, can we sit in a booth?" He didn't much like the look of the funny little tables and chairs. At least not for a boy to sit at.

Mrs. Morley said, "Anywhere you like."

The ice-cream parlor was almost deserted. They had their pick of the five booths, and Michael chose the one at the front. They could see the people passing on the street outside as they ate, and he liked that.

"What do you want to have?" Mrs. Morley drew off her gloves and laid them neatly over her handbag on the seat of the booth beside her. Michael and Queenie sat together opposite Mrs. Morley. Queenie's feet would not reach the floor and she kicked her shoes against the bottom of her booth seat. Mrs. Morley hoped she would not do that long.

"A chocolate soda," Michael decided promptly.

"Me too," said Queenie.

The waitress set down three glasses of water and took out a pad to write their order.

"Drink some water, little girl," Mrs. Morley directed. "It will help your hiccups while you're waiting for the ice cream."

To the waitress she said, "Two chocolate sodas and a lemonade."

Queenie drank some water and then began sucking on an ice cube.

"So you two are friends of Mrs. Poldini's?" Mrs. Morley asked.

"We live upstairs from her," Michael explained. "And we pass out her handbills. We gave you one."

"Were you the person who handed that to me? I'm afraid I didn't notice who gave it to me."

"It was me," Michael said proudly. "We get a penny apiece for handing them out."

"My!" Mrs. Morley tried to sound impressed. She wished there were some place this boy could wash his hands before he ate—and surely someone ought to comb the little girl's hair . . .

"We go out on Saturdays, and we usually have about twenty or twenty-five apiece," Michael explained. "Then we have money for stuff we need."

"I see," Mrs. Morley said politely. She could also see that they did not squander their money on soap or combs.

When the sodas came the children were silent, busy drinking the cold soda water and spooning at the ice cream. Queenie almost at once spilled a big glob of ice cream on the front of her dress. Mrs. Morley thought the boy was about twelve, the girl a year or two younger— ten, perhaps, and a far cry from Mrs. Morley's own Dorothea at the age of ten.

Even though Mrs. Morley's daughter had been grown a long time, Mrs. Morley had never ceased comparing other children she met with her own Dorothea. Dorothea had been a dainty, clean little girl, with long yellow curls. Any comparisons Mrs. Morley made with other little girls ended in Dorothea's favor. And certainly there was hardly any comparison at all between Dorothea, when she had been ten years old, and this skinned-kneed, scraggly-haired, hiccupy child sucking noisily on her soda straw. Dorothea never skinned her knees; her hiccups were very occasional and never loud; she kept her clothes clean, her hands washed, her socks pulled up at the heel. She took ballet lessons on Saturdays and piano lessons on Wednesdays. She always had a prominent part in school programs. Now that she was grown and married, she was a slender, immaculate beauty, and Mrs. Morley only hoped that Dorothea's husband appreciated her superiority over other women.

Mrs. Morley could not even wildly imagine Queenie as a grown-up woman. But she was glad to notice that the hiccups had stopped.

Queenie had not said anything since they met Mrs. Morley, but when she had reached the bottom of her soda glass and no amount of strenuous sucking at her straw could bring up another delicious drop, she looked up at Mrs. Morley from between two limp strands of hair and said,

"We saw your cat."

"My cat? Oh, India." Mrs. Morley made a face. "She's not *my* cat. Heaven forbid. She was my husband's cat."

"She came out of your house and ran under the bushes, and she wouldn't come out," Queenie said sadly.

"I wish she'd run away for good," Mrs. Morley said, making another face. "I never liked cats, and my husband *would* have them. That last one, before India—Butterfly he called her—really, that man had the craziest ideas about names—anyway, I thought she was going to live to be a hundred. Talk about nine lives! No more cats, I told him, when Butterfly finally died. And it wasn't a week before he'd brought home this miserable stray. She was only a kitten then, but you could tell she was going to be ugly. Thin, yellow—with those awful green eyes. And she wasn't even friendly. Scratched and hissed. How he could stand her I'll never know. And he named her India—well, really, there's no point talking about it. I'm going to get rid of her now, of course."

"Don't you want her?" Queenie's thin little face lit up. She felt Michael kick her under the table, but she didn't care. Hopeful desire was plain in her eyes.

Mrs. Morley could hardly believe her good fortune.

"How would *you* like to have India?" she said, with an air of munificence. "She can be your reward for returning my wallet—that and the ice cream."

Michael groaned inwardly again, this time for more reasons than one. His last hope of a few dollars' reward vanished, and now there was the added problem of the cat. Their mother wouldn't like a cat at all; he was quite sure of that.

"Oh, *could* I?" Queenie's face was radiant. She brushed her hair aside and dazzled Mrs. Morley with a radiant smile.

"Yes, of course, dear," Mrs. Morley crooned. "I'll be *happy* to give her to you. We can go back to my house and get her as soon as you've finished your ice cream."

"I finished."

Michael started to say something and then closed his mouth. Queenie looked so happy he just couldn't say what he wanted, that their mother probably wouldn't let her keep the cat. He knew he should say it now and save Queenie a lot of disappointment, but the words stuck in his throat.

Mrs. Morley, fearful lest something upset this wonderful plan if she did not hurry, was taking money out of her wallet as fast as she could. She turned impatiently to look around the shop, and caught the waitress's attention.

"May we have our check, please?"

Some great day this turned out to be, Michael thought glumly as he followed Mrs. Morley and Queenie out of the ice-cream shop. "Maybe you get reward, maybe not," Mrs. Poldini had said. Boy, was she ever right!

# *Family Argument*

As they approached Mrs. Morley's house they could see another car had parked beside the dark-blue sedan which had been in front of the house when Michael first tried to return the wallet. The second car was yellow with whitewall tires. It was freshly washed.

"Oh, dear," Mrs. Morley said with a sigh when she saw the car. "Arthur and Letitia are still here, and now Dorothea's come."

She frowned at the blue and yellow cars and glanced toward the house with a defeated expression.

"Haven't they turned things upside down enough already?" she asked.

Michael and Queenie stood beside her and looked at the two cars.

"There was a man here when we came with the wallet," Michael said. "But I didn't want to give it to him."

"Hmmm." Mrs. Morley's eyes narrowed. "That was my husband's brother Arthur. He and his wife came just before I went out. I hope Dorothea hasn't gotten into a row with them. Why do I have to have all this trouble!"

Then, remembering the children and her promise to Queenie, she said, "The cat's probably still outside here somewhere. We might as well look for her."

They took different directions in the yard calling, "Here, India—nice kitty," but no cat appeared. Mrs. Morley was tempted once to warn the children to be careful if they did find India, because India scratched. But on second thought she did not want to say anything to discourage them from taking the animal off her hands, so she went on around the yard crouching down to peer under the shubbery. She had some unpleasant thoughts about her dead husband, his cats, his stamp collection— and his dreadful will.

At last they gave up the search.

"Perhaps Dorothea let India in the house when she came," Mrs. Morley said. "There doesn't seem to be much point in looking out here anymore. Or perhaps she's run away."

"Oh, no," Queenie said mournfully. She had plans to have India sleep at the foot of her bed. She was going to take her for rides in her doll buggy, and maybe in the basket Michael sometimes put on the front of his bike.

Mrs. Morley patted the dejected little face. "If India has gone off, she'll be back when she gets hungry. But maybe she's in the house. We'll go and see."

The children followed Mrs. Morley up the front steps. The door was unlocked and Mrs. Morley opened it and told them to come into the hallway. Queenie hung back doubtfully. She did not want to see that big cross man again.

But she wanted to find India more, so at last she came in. Her hiccups started again and Mrs. Morley sighed. Ice cream had always worked with Dorothea's hiccups. But then, Dorothea had been such an exceptional girl.

The entrance hall was narrow and dark. It did nothing

to bolster Queenie's courage and she clung close to Michael. Almost at once they were greeted by the sound of angry voices coming from the living room off the hall, and Mrs. Morley sighed again.

"Well, into the fray," she said with resignation. "You children wait here a moment and then we'll see if we can find India."

She left them in the hallway and went into the living room. The tall, dark-browed man was there—Arthur Morley, brother of the dead George Morley. Michael and Queenie could see him pacing rapidly back and forth.

The newcomer, the owner of the yellow car, was Dorothea Dodd, Mrs. Morley's daughter. She was a slender, aloof-looking woman who kept adjusting the bracelets on her arm as she talked—and talking she was. A torrent of words filled the room.

". . . all those years Mother and I did without things, and Father sat around with his smelly old pipes, watching those darned baseball games on television. You have no right to be here, looking through Mother's things."

"Dorothea's right. You know perfectly well those stamps belong to me." Mrs. Morley joined the battle in midstream, but well aware of how things stood. "You have no right looking around my house, even if George did mention you in the will."

"But George *did* mention Arthur in the will—or anybody else who might find the stamps," a fourth voice chimed into the argument. An extremely fat little woman rose with a rustle from a chair across the room and moved toward the others to a point in the room where Michael and Queenie could see her from the hallway. This was Arthur's wife, Letitia, fat and shapeless, with a pink spot

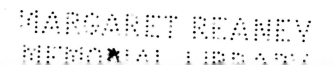

of rouge on each bloated cheek and a neck girdled with rolls of flesh. Like many fat people, she had extremely small hands and feet, and she teetered along on tiny shoes with high heels.

Queenie almost giggled when she saw her but was interrupted by a hiccup.

Mrs. Morley glanced at the fat woman irritably. "I don't care what George said. And I'm tired of having you poke around through everything." Turning back to Arthur, she added, "I suppose you'll be tearing up the floorboards next, or digging up the garden."

"That's not a bad idea," Arthur Morley answered hotly. His pacing brought him past the doorway, and he glared out at Michael and Queenie.

"You must have some idea where those stamps are, Amanda," Letitia Morley said accusingly. Her fat little chins quivered. "You were here with George all the time. I can't believe you really don't know where they are."

"Well, I don't," Mrs. Morley snapped.

"Maybe they aren't even here, Aunt Letitia," Dorothea said with a faintly amused smile. "Did you ever think of that?"

"Good heavens." Dorothea's mother threw up a hand in horror. "Don't even think such a thing, Dorothea. What will we have to do next, search the whole world?"

"Maybe you've already found them, for all we know," Arthur Morley declared.

"I certainly haven't," Mrs. Morley replied indignantly. "If I found them I'd let you know, you may be sure of that. It would end all this messing around."

"Then what was in that package you had yesterday, I'd like to know?"

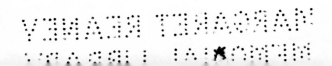

"What package?" Mrs. Morley snapped back angrily, without stopping to think.

"What package?" Arthur Morley repeated mockingly.

"What package?" Dorothea wanted to know too.

"I don't know anything about any package," Mrs. Morley protested.

"Listen to that," Mr. Morley shouted. "Just listen to that."

"There is no need to shout at me," Mrs. Morley answered coldly.

"Whatever is he talking about, Mother?"

"Tell them, Arthur," Letitia said. Her fat face glowed with satisfaction.

"I'll tell you what package," Arthur Morley went on, still shouting. "That square, flat package you had yesterday when you went to Hopkins Street. Just the right size for a stamp album."

"You followed me!" Mrs. Morley shrieked with vexation.

"Now who's shouting?" Letitia wanted to know.

Mrs. Morley made an effort to control her emotions. "I'd like to know what business you have following me around, Arthur Morley."

"And I'd like to know what was in that package."

"It was *not* the stamp album," Mrs. Morley replied quickly—but here she floundered. How could she tell them she had been foolish enough to consult a spiritualist to contact George. That she had taken a photograph of George. How they would ridicule her for such a thing.

"That package is none of your business," she concluded, drawing herself up with dignity. "I'd still like to know what you are doing sneaking around after me."

"And I'd still like to know what you had in that package."

"You'll be tearing up the floorboards next." Mrs. Morley went back to her former argument. Anything to get Arthur off the subject of that package and the building on Hopkins Street.

"Good idea," he said angrily.

"And digging up the garden," Mrs. Morley continued heatedly. Her face was flushed with the exertion of the combat with Arthur.

"Good. Just give me a shovel and I'll start now."

"I bet you would," Mrs. Morley replied. Her flush deepened. "I just bet you would—you—you greedy old— old—" Further appropriate words failed her.

"Come, come, Mother," Dorothea said nervously. "You two are behaving like children. Uncle Arthur isn't going to tear up any floorboards—"

"Children—oh, dear," Mrs. Morley interrupted Dorothea. "I forgot the children. And we've been making such a racket."

She stepped to the doorway and tried to smile at Michael and Queenie as though nothing unusual had occurred.

"I'll be with you two in a moment."

Then she went back into the living room and they could hear her saying, "There are two children here. They've come to take India."

"Good," Dorothea said, adjusting her bracelets.

"I couldn't agree more," Mrs. Morley replied. "That's one less problem I'll have. But we can't find her."

"I'm getting out of this place," Arthur Morley decided abruptly. "Come along, Letitia."

He came storming out of the room and brushed rudely past Michael and Queenie. Queenie hiccuped furiously and Michael whispered, "Can't you be more quiet, for Pete's sake."

Out of the living room came Letitia Morley, springing along on her high heels, her fat little body shaking.

"Hello," she said to the children absently as she teetered by.

"The cat's around someplace," Dorothea was saying, as the front door slammed loudly behind the departing Arthur and Letitia Morley. "I let her in when I came."

Dorothea came out into the hall with Mrs. Morley and stood looking with disapproval at Michael and Queenie. She thought untidy children were very unappealing. Didn't that little girl mind all that hair hanging in her face? Well, India would probably scratch them to pieces, if they found her and really did take her home. India was the meanest cat Dorothea had ever seen.

Mrs. Morley did not bother with introductions, and Dorothea Dodd went out and down the porch stairs and drove away in her clean yellow car, to her clean magazine-picture house and her tidy husband, an elegant man, quite unlike Dorothea's poor father. Mr. Dodd did not smoke smelly pipes or watch baseball games, or pick up stray cats or collect stamps.

Mrs. Morley took off her hat. She felt limp. Arguments always left her limp and weak. Arthur Morley had been a cross she had had to bear all her married life. George hadn't liked him either. And Letitia was just as bad— Letitia in her green dress, like a round head of lettuce.

As she stood staring at the two children waiting in the hallway, a thought crossed Mrs. Morley's somewhat agitated mind. So many places around the house had been looked through, hunting for the stamps; but sometimes something obvious escaped the most vigorous searchers. Here were two fresh minds to bring to the problem. Children were supposed to be intuitive, Mrs. Morley had always heard. Something might occur to them that would never occur to the grown-ups.

"We've been looking for a stamp album," she began, feeling her way cautiously and watching the children's faces as she talked.

Of course, Michael and Queenie knew all about the strange will and the missing stamps from Mrs. Poldini, but they stared back blankly at Mrs. Morley, giving no sign at all that they had ever heard of these stamps.

Mrs. Morley sat down on the hall steps and stretched her legs. She eased off her shoes and sighed with the comfort this brought.

"My husband had a large and rather valuable stamp collection, and he died without . . . without remembering to tell me where he had put it. We've looked everywhere we can think of. We've taken everything out of all the closets and cupboards. We've looked in the attic and the basement and—well, just everywhere we can think of."

Michael and Queenie waited silently. Queenie wanted her cat. Then she wanted to go home.

Michael was thinking maybe he could earn a reward after all. The day was not over. Maybe he could find Mrs. Morley's stamps and get a reward for that. "Maybe you get reward, maybe not," Mrs. Poldini had warned him. Well, there was still a chance.

"I bet we could find the stamps," Michael spoke up

at last. "Queenie and me are real good at finding things —aren't we, Queenie."

He poked Queenie and she hiccuped.

"Before we start looking, I think you'd better have a drink of water, little girl." Mrs. Morley put her shoes on again and stood up. She took Queenie's hand. "What *is* your name, by the way?"

"It's Queenie," Michael answered for her. "And I'm Michael."

"All right, Queenie," Mrs. Morley said. "Come and have some water, and then we'll find the cat—and maybe the stamps. Wouldn't that be nice?"

Michael followed Mrs. Morley and Queenie toward the kitchen. No, the day was not over yet, he assured himself.

# Eight:
## Searching

India came shooting out from under the kitchen table. "There you are!" Mrs. Morley scolded.

The cat stood in the middle of the kitchen floor, its tail high. It did not look very friendly.

"Get out of the way," Mrs. Morley commanded. When she went to the cupboard India was right at her heels.

"Can't take a step without that cat in the way," she said, but then she cut herself short. She did not want to discourage the children from taking India.

"Nice kitty," she said more pleasantly. "I guess she's just hungry."

Mrs. Morley opened the refrigerator door and took out an open can of cat food, half eaten. It was wrapped in wax paper, and the cat began to push against Mrs. Morley's ankles as she unwrapped the paper.

"Can't you wait a minute?" she said to it. "There."

Michael and Queenie watched as Mrs. Morley set out the cat's supper. The can clattered on the linoleum and the cat sprang toward it eagerly. But after nosing at it a bit, it turned back to Mrs. Morley, meowing.

"Fussy, fussy," Mrs. Morley rebuked. To Michael and Queenie she said, "Won't eat it if it's cold. Spoiled rotten. George always did that with his cats. He cooked special things for India sometimes, but I can't go to all that bother with all the other things I have to do."

She ran water at the sink and got a glass for Queenie.

When she handed the water to Queenie, Queenie shook her head.

"My hiccups stopped," she said.

Truly an exasperating little girl, Mrs. Morley thought.

"Well, you might as well drink the water anyway, now that I've got it. Keep them from coming back."

Obediently Queenie took the glass and drank the water. She felt as if her hiccups might start again, but she didn't think she ought to mention this to Mrs. Morley. Mrs. Morley looked rather cross.

"Now why don't you children look around," Mrs. Morley said when Queenie had finished her water and was trying not to hiccup again. "We can go upstairs in the attic. And there's the basement." She tried to make it sound like a game. "Something just might *come* to you, you know."

"Like a vision," Michael suggested.

"Exactly," Mrs. Morley agreed. "Like a vision."

Michael and Queenie wandered through the upstairs of Mrs. Morley's house, hoping for a vision, through the stuffy dark attic, through three bedrooms that looked as if they had already been well searched. Then they came down to the first floor again.

Somewhere along the way they were joined by India, who kept springing up on places she shouldn't be. Mrs. Morley kept saying, "Get off that bed . . . get down from that bureau . . ." In the dining room she said, "Get off that *table*."

As she led the way down the steps to the basement,

Mrs. Morley said, "I'm afraid Arthur and Letitia have already thought of all the good hiding places. It will be just my luck for them to find the album first."

The basement had once upon a time been very neat. Both Amanda Morley and her late husband George had been orderly people. Mr. Morley's tools had hung on a pegboard along one wall. Nearby, there was a shelf with an orderly row of jars containing screws and nails and bolts of various sizes.

The washing machine and laundry tubs were set apart from this workshop section.

Some used pieces of furniture had been stored on one side of the basement, and in another section there were garden tools and some folding chairs brought in from the yard now that summer was over.

But signs of searching were evident here in the basement as well as in the other rooms in the house. The tools had been removed from the pegboard, and the pegboard itself taken down from the wall. Cushions in the furniture had been removed Drawers had been opened. Newspapers once neatly stacked had been shuffled through and replaced haphazardly.

"Such a mess," Mrs. Morley said to herself dejectedly.

India had followed them down and curled herself on one of the piles of newspaper. Queenie went over to her and tried to pet her, but the cat reached out a paw and would have scratched her hand if Queenie had not been quick enough to draw it out of the way first.

But Queenie was not daunted because India seemed unfriendly. It was only because the poor kitty had to live in this unfriendly house with all these yelling people. And she looked so thin, as if nobody had fed her very much or very often.

"I'm going to take you home with me," Queenie said to the cat softly. Michael and Mrs. Morley were in the back of the basement looking through boxes of garden tools— for the umpteenth time, Mrs. Morley admitted to herself, but she looked anyway for lack of any other ideas of where to look.

Then, staring into the green eyes of the yellow cat, Queenie thought of something that had not occurred to Mrs. Morley, or Arthur Morley, or his plump wife, or the immaculate Dorothea Dodd. Or even to Michael. It occurred to Queenie that India knew where those stamps were. India had been Mr. Morley's special pet. She had probably followed him around everywhere. She had probably been watching when he hid the stamps.

Queenie gazed into the cat's eyes.

"Where are the stamps, India?" she whispered into the cat's face. Its whiskers bristled, but it did not answer.

Cautiously Queenie put out her hand once more, and when the cat did not seem to want to scratch again, she put out her other hand and boldly lifted the cat from the newspapers. It hung like a dead thing in her hands, its feet dangling almost to the floor, its tail swishing slowly.

"Show me where they are," Queenie whispered into the cat's ear. This bothered India and she wriggled to get free. Queenie put her on the floor. "Now you show me," she said, "and I'll follow you."

To her delight the cat began nosing around at one of the folding chairs, and Queenie crouched on the floor and peered under the chair, which lay flat upon the floor. She put her hand underneath, but there was nothing there but the cold concrete of the floor.

India bolted away, up the stairs to the kitchen. Queenie followed. Nobody noticed her going.

In the kitchen the cat nosed the half-eaten can of cat food a moment or two, and then leaped onto the table.

"Show me, India, darling," Queenie coaxed.

The cat leaped to the floor again, and this time went to the back door. It stood with its back arched and began to meow.

Queenie opened the door. There was a screen door, and she opened that too.

The cat looked up at her.

"Go on—show me," Queenie said again. She bent down toward the cat, hair hanging in her eyes.

The cat walked out on the back porch. And Queenie was close behind.

The backyard was covered with fallen leaves. By a fence at the end of the yard a row of rosebushes had long since seen their last blossom of that season. In the alley, garbage cans were set out for the morning pickup. In the yard next door two boys were playing ball, and a smaller boy was riding from a swing attached to a tree branch.

India ran down the steps and around the side of the house. When Queenie caught up with her she was scratching in the dirt by a row of four-o'clock bushes.

Queenie stood and watched.

"Is that where the stamps are—buried in the bushes?" she asked the cat.

A warm prickly feeling of success enveloped her as she watched the cat dig farther and farther back into the bushes. She had found where the stamps were. India had shown her!

## Nine:

# *India*

"I suppose it's possible," Mrs. Morley said doubtfully. "Anything's possible . . . but still, oh, I just don't know."

Queenie had brought Michael and Mrs. Morley outside to the yard and showed them the place where India had been scratching under the bushes.

"She could have been chasing a mouse or something," Mrs. Morley said. She stood frowning down at the bushes.

"I really wasn't serious when I asked Arthur if he wanted to dig up the garden. Still, there might be something to it. But if George did bury his stamps out here . . ." Her gaze wandered reflectively around the yard. ". . . if he did, it would seem more likely to me to look in the flower bed. That was where he was always puttering around."

Over at the side of the yard, Michael and Queenie could see a circular area laid out with tiny stones. The summer flowers were long gone, but a few clumps and stalks remained, partly buried by the fallen autumn leaves.

"I could dig it up for you," Michael offered.

"Oh—it just seems too foolish, even for George." Mrs. Morley shook her head fretfully. "I still think the stamps are somewhere in the house, probably in the basement."

"You'd better go back and see Mrs. Poldini," Michael suggested.

Mrs. Morley did not answer at once. She continued to look at the bedraggled flower bed. Then she said, "Perhaps I will. Who knows."

Her attention returned to the children, and she was dismayed to see that Queenie—who had not been too neat to begin with—was now in even worse condition. Above her skinned knees, clumps of damp earth and twigs clung to her dress where it had brushed the ground when she crawled in under the bushes to see what India was digging at. A barrette which had held back some of her flying hair had slid down and was hanging by only a few strands. A smear of dirt where she had rubbed her face extended from her chin to her ear.

Well, it is her mother's problem, Mrs. Morley thought. But even so, she brushed at Queenie's dress and managed to get off the worst of the dirt and twigs. She took out the barrette and clasped it up higher into Queenie's hair. The child still looked dreadful, but Mrs. Morley's energy was declining.

"We've looked enough for today," she said. Suddenly she was tired. Her head began to ache, a delayed reaction from that silly squabble with Arthur, no doubt. She wanted to be alone, to have a cup of hot chocolate and take her shoes off and just sit.

Queenie was disappointed. She had thought everybody would be excited to hear that India had run almost straight to the bushes when she asked about the stamps. She had thought the whole mystery would be solved.

"I've got some cat food in the house you might as well take if you're going to take the cat," Mrs. Morley said wearily and led the way back into the kitchen.

First she brought down an old hat box from a closet upstairs, for Queenie to carry India in. And then from the kitchen pantry she got a good-sized carton of cat food in small tin cans. Some of the cans in the top layer were missing—as Mrs. Morley had been grudgingly forced to feed India now and then during the week since George had died and was no longer able to take care of *his* cat. When Michael saw they were going to get some free cat food he thought this might make his mother more willing to have a cat—but not much, probably. Still, it was something.

Michael put the carton on his shoulder (which gave him a rather swaggering feeling), and Mrs. Morley stuffed India into the hat box. This was not done without considerable objection from India, who succeeded in giving Mrs. Morley one last good-bye scratch.

"You beast," Mrs. Morley said to it, clutching her finger to her mouth. Then she clamped down the hat box cover and tied the cord that held it in place.

"I wouldn't carry the box by the cord, if I were you," she said, taking the hat box up carefully in both hands and passing it down to Queenie. "The cat's pretty heavy. You better just hold the box in your arms."

Queenie hiccuped suddenly, a fitting end to a disturbing afternoon, Mrs. Morley thought. And it did not take her two minutes once the children had gone to have her shoes off and her hot chocolate warming on the stove.

It did not take India two minutes to get out of the hat box. As they started down the street Queenie only lifted the lid a tiny, tiny bit to peek in at her treasure, and that was enough. India's head came through like a bolt of lightning, and although her body did not follow so quickly

—indeed took considerable wriggling and clawing—she was soon halfway out.

"Hey, Queenie, watch what you're doing," Michael warned. But too late. Queenie had to make a choice of holding on to either India or the hat box—and she chose India. Seizing the cat in a grip made firm by desperation, Queenie let go of the hat box, which clattered away, landed on its side, and began to roll jauntily down the street. Michael made a grab at it, but he really needed both hands to steady the carton on his shoulder.

In the meantime India was squirming and struggling to get away from Queenie.

"Come on, let's run," Michael shouted, and they began to stumble along home as fast as they could. But it could not be called much of a run.

At the intersection of their own block a passing car honked at them loudly as they fled in front of it, and at the sound of the horn the cat gave one terrified lunge and came out of Queenie's arms right up the front of her dress and onto her head. There it clung with its claws in Queenie's hair, and no amount of tugging and pulling from either Queenie or Michael would loosen its grip.

"Hold still, Queenie!" Michael had set down the carton, but he could not get a good grasp of the cat.

"You're hurting me," Queenie wailed.

The cat thrashed its tail against Michael's arm and across Queenie's forehead.

"Oh, oh, oh!" Queenie wailed again, hiding her face in her hands. "You're pulling my hair, Michael; you're pulling my hair."

A woman driving by in a car looked at them curiously, but she was in a hurry and could not stop to help.

"Oh, oh, oh!" Queenie began to jump up and down.

At last Michael had to give up.

He had hoped to present India to their mother in the best possible light, but there did not seem anything to do now but go upstairs the way they were, with the cat clinging to Queenie's head. Boy, this is never going to work, Michael said to himself over and over as they went up the stairs. This is never going to work in a million years.

When Mrs. Allen saw Queenie with the cat on her head she gave a cry of alarm, and the children's hasty explanations went largely unheard as their mother tried to disentangle the cat. The problem turned out to be the barrette, which Mrs. Morley had refastened more securely on Queenie's hair. One of the cat's claws had caught in it. When this was discovered, things went more easily and Queenie was soon rubbing at her pulled hair while India ran under the sofa to hide.

Then Michael told the story again—about returning Mrs. Morley's wallet and how, her husband being dead, she didn't want his cat anymore.

Perhaps it was because the baby had not cried all day and Mrs. Allen's spirits were up, or perhaps it was the sight of the free cat food or Queenie's radiantly hopeful eyes—dear little Queenie, Mrs. Allen thought, with a pang for all the cross words she had ever said to the little girl . . . she was really so good, no trouble at all most of the time . . . and she seemed to want the cat so very much.

At any rate, Mrs. Allen's reception of the cat was more than Michael had dared to hope for.

"Well, we might try it," his mother said.

"She'll probably spend a lot of time downstairs with

Mrs. Poldini," Michael said, hoping by this to more or less clinch the whole matter. "Mrs. Poldini likes cats."

"That's an idea," Mrs. Allen said, with more charity than she usually showed when she mentioned Mrs. Poldini's name. "That might work out."

"Can I keep it?" That was all Queenie wanted to know.

"For a while—we'll see how it works out," Mrs. Allen said. For a moment a cloud of uneasiness crossed her face. She hoped Michael wouldn't start pestering her for a dog again because Queenie had a cat. But Michael seemed contented about the cat. He was lying on his stomach by the couch trying to coax India to come out.

Queenie opened a can of cat food and lay down beside Michael on the floor. She shoved the can close to India's nose, and step by step India came out from under the couch to have her supper.

"She doesn't like it cold," Queenie explained to her mother.

"Is that right?"

Mrs. Allen wished the cat had at least been a pretty one. If they had to have a cat at all, she would have liked one of those Siamese cats with the cunning faces. This cat was ugly, even for a cat.

As soon as India had eaten, Michael and Queenie dragged her downstairs to show Mrs. Poldini.

Mrs. Poldini had drawn her shades for evening and sat alone in a solitary ring of lamplight. On the round purple-covered table she had laid the photograph of George Morley, face up. She was studying it intently, the lids half closed over her dark and mysterious eyes.

<h1>Ten:</h1>
<h1>*Mrs. Poldini*</h1>

Mrs. Poldini listened to Michael's story about returning the wallet and helping Mrs. Morley look for the stamp album. Her lids drooped over her eyes. Her expression became more gloomy. Now and then she would gaze mournfully at the thin yellow cat in Queenie's arms.

"Some reward," Michael concluded. But he didn't really feel as bad as he had. Having a cat was better than nothing—although not better than having a dog.

"Michael told her to come back and see you," Queenie said.

She stood close beside Mrs. Poldini's chair, leaning her thin little body against the faded velour. Her trust in Mrs. Poldini's powers was complete. If Mrs. Morley would only return, Queenie was sure beyond any doubt that Mrs. Poldini could contact Mr. Morley from the beyond.

"She sure needs *some* help, with that guy searching all over her house," Michael said. "Boy, is he mean-looking. I'd like to find those stamps for Mrs. Morley just to show him!"

"Maybe she come back, maybe not," Mrs. Poldini said.

When Queenie went to bed that night, she made a deep round spot on the foot of her bed for India. Standing in her bare feet and wearing a pair of outgrown pajamas, she pressed the cat down into the blanket. But it was not as easy as she had thought it would be. India

71

did not want to go to bed. Her green eyes were wary, her tail thrashed.

"You can sleep here by me," Queenie crooned to the cat lovingly. She put her face down by the cat's and stared into the green eyes.

"Where are the stamps, India? Are they in the flower bed? Tell me . . ."

India glared back and tried to wriggle away. Queenie felt her fingers losing their grip, and though she tried to tighten her hold India slipped free and jumped down from the bed.

"Oh, come back, India," Queenie cried. But the unwilling creature fled under the bed.

Queenie knelt beside the bed and reached her arm under into the darkness. India raked it with a scratch.

Queenie sat back on her heels and rubbed her arm. Tears flooded her eyes, but she wiped them away. India would soon get used to her, she was sure, and then she would come up some night and sleep at the foot of the bed.

"Good night, kitty," Queenie said at last.

She got into bed and pulled up the covers. But then, one last time she hung over the edge of the bed, head first, hair streaming nearly to the floor. By lifting the hem of the sheet she could see under the bed, where two spots of light glowed in the darkness. Into those unfathomable eyes Queenie gazed intently for a long time. India knew where the stamps were, Queenie was sure. Someday she would tell.

Downstairs, Mrs. Poldini sat alone in the darkening night. Her teakettle hissed softly in the kitchen, filling the rooms with a misty vapor. There was not another sound. No radio played, no baby cried. As the night lengthened, the stillness grew. Finally there was no one awake in the whole apartment building except Mrs. Poldini.

Her thought, concentrated at first on the dead Mr. Morley, came to rest eventually on what Queenie had said. "I know you can help her," Queenie had said as she left with her yellow cat. Her eyes, upturned to Mrs. Poldini's brooding face, had been implicitly trustful. Nothing was impossible to Mrs. Poldini.

Yet now, in the darkness and stillness that surrounded her, Mrs. Poldini was admitting to herself, as she sometimes did in the darkness on lonely nights, that she was nothing but a fake. Ah, it was true.

Years and years ago there had been a friend of Mrs. Poldini's mother who claimed to be a spiritualist, and just as Queenie and Michael now hung with unabating interest upon everything Mrs. Poldini told them about contacting the dead, about reading palms, reading minds, and reading tea leaves, so Mrs. Poldini as a child had listened to her mother's friend. This woman had been a thin old hag with scrawny arms and untended hair. Her bony hands caressed a crystal ball, clutched a palm to read the lines, rattled teacup against saucer as she peered into the depths of the unknown and read the future in the formation of the tea leaves.

"Someone is calling to me from the beyond," she had cried one day, and the little girl who was now Mrs. Poldini had drawn closer that she too might hear the voice from the beyond and share the secrets.

And then one long-ago night some tree-branch shadow by her window had mingled in her half-awakeness to take the shape of a head. She had been dreaming of her dead grandfather, and as she looked, the shadow seemed more and more like him. Still half asleep, she had stared at this ghostly presence until she believed it was true. And because he was there, he must speak to her, she thought, speak to her from the beyond.

"Ahhhhhh," the old friend of her mother's had sighed when she heard the story the next day. "You have the power as I do, my child, to reveal the secrets of the unknown."

And she had patted the head of the small dark-eyed girl who stood close to her chair and believed everything she said.

When she was grown, Mrs. Poldini had married The Great Poldini, a magician with a circus.

His talent had been a true talent. Things appeared and disappeared magically under his touch. The children in the circus audience never tired of watching his performance, sitting forward on the edges of their seats, agog with wonder as six doves flew from an empty box and then flew in again—a moment before the box itself ceased to exist before their widened eyes.

Mrs. Poldini had liked her years with the circus. She still kept the ancient spangled dresses and still wore the earrings and bracelets she had worn then, when she was Madame Mysterio, with her own bright tent and a crystal ball even larger than the thin old crone's had been. She had learned just what to say to mystify and please the customers, farm girls who came in giggling while their beaux lingered by the outer flap of the tent, farm wives who wanted to be told a good year lay ahead for them, children who hung over the crystal ball closer than Mrs. Poldini herself, and breathed on it with their small red mouths.

Sometimes, staring into the glass ball, Mrs. Poldini would cry as the old woman had cried, "Someone is calling to me from the beyond."

How the customers had shivered with joy and dread.

But by and by, when The Great Poldini himself had gone beyond, Mrs. Poldini had taken up a quieter life. Now she was old and tired, and only her fading circus dresses remained to remind her of those long-gone days. Now she supported herself by reading tea leaves in The Red Moon Tea Shop three afternoons and three evenings a week and by passing out her handbills advertising her powers to probe the mysteries of the universe.

But she knew she was a fake, that the whole world of crystal balls, palm reading, tea leaves, visions, vibrations, and visitations was as substanceless as the air. There was no telling the future or talking to the dead. Mrs. Morley would have to find the stamps by herself, of course. Well, then, life is a difficult business at best. . . .

Sighing wearily, Mrs. Poldini rose at last and shuffled to her cluttered bedroom. She turned on a light and stood blinking dismally at the sudden glare. Then she began to look amidst her forty pairs of shoes for a particular pair of bedroom slippers. She found only the left one and put it on sadly. Even in small matters, life was difficult. She wished some mystic powers would show her where the missing slipper was, but she did not waste any time on it.

Nor, when she had drunk her bedtime cup of tea, did she spend more than a moment contemplating the formation of the leaves in the bottom of the cup. They told her only that Mrs. Morley was on her own and that it was time for bed.

PART THREE

# MESSAGE FROM THE BEYOND

# Eleven

# Mrs. Morley Returns

However, we must all eat, Mrs. Poldini reminded herself the next morning. She readied herself to contact the beyond, if Mrs. Morley should return.

It was a cold day. Winter was coming. No ray of sunlight found its way between the buildings and into the shabby street where Mrs. Poldini lived. As the day progressed and Mrs. Morley did not come, Mrs. Poldini sat at her window and watched the street. At three o'clock she boiled some cabbage and ate it in her steamy little kitchen. Upstairs the baby began to cry again. Mrs. Poldini finished her cabbage and listened to the crying.

At four o'clock Mrs. Morley arrived. She had gotten out a heavier coat to wear, and her cheeks were pink from walking in the cold wind. She was thinking that if winter came it would be hard indeed to find anything buried in the garden.

"You are absolutely my last hope," Mrs. Morley said.

Mrs. Poldini had drawn the curtains, and the two were seated at the round table. As before, the photograph of George Morley lay between them on the table, and Mrs. Poldini had already placed her hands upon it, as she had done the time before.

Mrs. Morley drew off her gloves and put her own fingers on the photograph. She was surprised to feel that her fingers were shaking and as cold as ice.

"Today I feel we succeed," Mrs. Poldini announced in a somber tone.

Mrs. Morley opened her mouth slightly. It seemed that as Mrs. Poldini spoke, the photograph stirred beneath her fingers. But it was probably only the trembling of her own hands.

Mrs. Poldini's dark eyes closed. Fully and finally, she sat trapped behind the closed eyes, motionless as death.

It seemed to Mrs. Morley that a long, long time passed. Upstairs she could hear someone walking around. And once, from somewhere outside in the apartment hallway, a door banged loudly and there were voices for a few moments, though no words were distinguishable.

At last, when Mrs. Morley felt she could not bear to sit so tensely another moment, Mrs. Poldini began to speak.

Her voice was hardly more than a whisper, and Mrs. Morley was forced to lean forward and strain her ears to hear.

"Someone . . . someone is calling to me . . . from the beyond."

Mrs. Morley wanted to ask if it was George, but she found that her mouth was quite dry and she could not say a word.

There was a short silence, during which Mrs. Poldini rocked slowly from side to side. Her earrings reflected the shadowy light that crept through the drawn curtains. Mrs. Morley was fascinated by the great inscrutable face across the table—and at the same time she became aware that Mrs. Poldini's hands were pressing down hard upon the photograph, drawing it closer to herself.

"Yes . . . we are ready." Mrs. Poldini spoke, not to Mrs. Morley, but into the beyond where the dead were.

"Is this George Morley? Answer me . . . yes, yes, your wife is here . . ."

Another interminable silence followed.

"A message is coming . . ."

Mrs. Morley drew in her breath. Her whole body was as rigid as a pole, but her fingers still trembled violently upon the edge of the photograph.

"Is she well? . . . your wife, you mean? . . ."

Then Mrs. Poldini spoke to Mrs. Morley: "Your husband wishes to know if you are well."

Mrs. Morley was surprised. In all their years of marriage George had rarely inquired about her health. He was considerably concerned with his own health, often declaring that he had palpitations of the heart, poor digestion, pains in his back, and a bad liver. He had taken for granted that his wife never suffered similar complaints. She never stayed in bed. She never went out even as far as the local grocery store without dressing so completely—earrings, gloves, a dab of cologne behind each ear—that she might meet any of her church ladies, or the minister himself, with the ease which comes from not being caught untidy or unpresentable. She scorned women who rushed out for a loaf of bread without lipstick or with curlers in their hair. Mrs. Morley cleaned on Tuesdays and Saturdays. She did the laundry and ironing on Mondays. She never missed church or her Friday-afternoon club meetings. She was never sick.

"Yes—yes, tell him I am well," Mrs. Morley stammered, somewhat impatient with George that now, after all these years, when she had so many more important things on her mind, he should be asking about her health.

"Tell Dorothea to be a good girl," Mrs. Poldini whispered.

She paused, as though waiting for a further message.

". . . and tell my brother he is a fool."

"I will, I will," Mrs. Morley assured Mrs. Poldini. She found that she was whispering too. It did not seem right to talk to the departed in any other way.

The shadows deepened in the room. Outside in the street a car passed occasionally. Some children ran by, shouting to each other through the cold wind.

"Ask George about the stamps," Mrs. Morley urged. She did not want George to fade away again before her real purpose was accomplished. Her health was as perfect as ever, Dorothea was always a good girl, and she would be glad to tell Arthur Morley he was a fool. But what she really wanted to know about was the stamps, that was the important thing.

"A message comes," Mrs. Poldini warned. Her eyes remained closed, her body swayed.

At last she spoke again,

"Look in your heart."

Mrs. Morley waited, but Mrs. Poldini said nothing further.

Finally Mrs. Morley whispered, "Is that all . . . is that all the message? Where are the stamps . . . oh, don't talk to me in riddles, George. . . ."

"Look in your heart," Mrs. Poldini said again.

"But what does that mean?" Mrs. Morley asked with agitation. "Ask him what he means. . . ."

But abruptly Mrs. Poldini's eyes flew open. They glimmered in the shadows, large and dark and full of mystery.

"He is gone," she said simply.

"Gone—what do you mean, gone? . . . He *can't* be. He hasn't told me anything. . . ." Mrs. Morley half rose from her chair. "Get him back."

"He is gone. He not return."

Mrs. Morley gasped. "But he *can't* be gone . . . he *can't* be . . ."

"He is gone."

Mrs. Morley sank back in her chair. She forgot how cold she had felt, for a hot anger swept over her now.

"And that's all he said?" She moaned with the sheer exasperation of it all. It was just like George. He had always been a stubborn, selfish man. He and his cats and his stamps and his smelly pipes! Now, when she really needed to *know* something, he was acting like this!

"He is gone." Mrs. Poldini stood up heavily. She went to the window and drew the curtain aside. Outside, the street lamps had come on. Twilight was falling.

"You mean he's gone for now? Perhaps another time . . ." Mrs. Morley clung to hope.

But Mrs. Poldini shook her head. She gazed down into the street. "He is gone forever."

"*Forever*—oh, he can't do this to me. . . ."

"Sometimes that is the way. Only once do the dead speak to us. Then they not return again."

"But he didn't *tell* me anything." Mrs. Morley felt her control slipping. She had counted so much on Mrs. Poldini and on George. They had both let her down. She was no better off than ever!

"Sometimes that is the way," Mrs. Poldini repeated.

She turned and looked down at the distraught Mrs. Morley. Her eyes revealed nothing.

"I am sorry. He not return. It is for you to think what he has said. You have message. Now you must understand."

"Understand!" Mrs. Morley rose now too, drawing on her gloves with angry, jerky motions quite unlike her usually careful treatment of her gloves. "What is there to understand?"

"All is revealed . . . mysteries of the universe . . ." Mrs. Poldini chanted, holding her arms out suddenly, as though to receive these mysteries at that very moment.

But Mrs. Morley was not listening. She yanked open her handbag and took out her wallet. Her lips were set in a pinched line. She took out a five-dollar bill and slapped it down on the table, right on the photograph.

"Good-bye," she said to Mrs. Poldini. "And you can keep that wretched picture for all I care, too."

Mrs. Poldini was still standing by the window when Mrs. Morley went out and slammed the door behind her.

A minute or so later Mrs. Poldini could see her marching away up the street toward home at a furious pace, a cold wind tugging at her coat, her handbag bouncing along at her side.

## Twelve:
# *Michael's Idea*

Saturday and Sunday passed quietly. Mrs. Morley did not return to reclaim her photograph of George Morley, and Mrs. Poldini put it on the top of her piano, amid a great clutter of other possessions. He smiled out from between a blue vase of plastic roses and an alarm clock that did not work.

Mrs. Poldini sat in The Red Moon Tea Shop, eyelids drooping, listening to the music of violins and observing the customers from her half-closed eyes. She sat at tables with them and gazed into their teacups at the fragments of sodden tea leaves and promised them trips across the water and romances with handsome dark, men. When no one was looking (for it was not allowed by her employers), she slipped copies of her handbills to the ladies with the teacups.

### CALL BACK THE DEAD

*Speak to your loved ones who have gone beyond*
*Receive messages from them*

*Mrs. Poldini can reveal to you the secrets of the unknown*

*712 Hopkins Street*

"Oh, my, doesn't that sound exciting," a lady would say to her companion. "We must try it sometime."

"All will be revealed. Mysteries of the unknown," Mrs. Poldini promised them.

"Oh, really?"

And the ladies would be whispering together as Mrs. Poldini rose and moved on from their table to another, swaying slightly to the melancholy rhythm of the violins.

Over the weekend Queenie and Michael tried to tame India and also to fatten her up. The cat had not been so well taken care of since Mr. Morley died, and she followed everyone around, rubbing against their ankles whenever she heard the refrigerator door opening. Queenie gave her three cans of cat food on Saturday, and three more on Sunday.

"I never saw an animal eat so much," Queenie's mother said. Her humor was considerably better now that the baby had stopped fussing.

When Mr. Allen came home from the garage, he gave Queenie a string with a bell attached, and she played with India by drawing the string along the carpet, tinkling the bell, until the cat sprang upon it, snarling the string and chewing at the bell.

On Saturday afternoon Michael and Queenie went along the streets passing out Mrs. Poldini's handbills, cheeks red with cold. Queenie's mother had made her put on a sweater that was itchy, and Queenie sniffled and hiccuped and scratched at her sweater until Michael said she was no help at all.

But on Sunday the weather turned warmer. Michael repaired the broken pedal on his bike and went for a long bike ride by himself Sunday afternoon. He thought about Mrs. Morley and the missing stamps—and he felt sure if he could have the freedom to search Mrs. Morley's house for a day or two, he would surely find the stamps.

There might be a reward for that, all right!

("Maybe you get reward," Mrs. Poldini had said. "Maybe not.")

Finding a stamp album worth twenty-five thousand dollars was certainly worth something, even if returning a wallet with twenty-two dollars and forty-six cents hadn't been. Or so it seemed to Michael.

What he wanted to think of was some perfectly simple hiding place where no one had thought to look. But as he was riding along that Sunday afternoon, no good ideas came to him. It was just before he went to bed that night that he had his idea. And then of course it was too late to do anything about it. And the next morning was Monday—school again; there was nothing to do but wait until after school.

"School takes up your whole life," he said begrudgingly to Queenie as they set out Monday morning. "I'm going back to Mrs. Morley's as soon as school's out. I want to look around that house some more."

"Can I go too?"

"If you want to," Michael answered with an offhand manner. But he was glad Queenie wanted to come along; he wanted as many people as possible to be there when he made "the great discovery." Boy, would they all be surprised.

After school the two set off for Mrs. Morley's. Michael rode his bike and Queenie sat on the handlebars, an arrangement that would have sent Mrs. Allen into a faint if she could have seen them wobbling along in this precarious manner. Fortunately, Mrs. Allen was safely at home taking a nap, so she was saved a lot of worry.

They turned down Mrs. Morley's block, and even from a distance they could see the dark-blue car that belonged to Arthur Morley parked at the curb.

"That guy has to be here," Michael said with disgust.

As they came closer to the house they could see that Arthur Morley and Mrs. Amanda Morley were out in the yard. There was no sign of the plump Letitia (she being at that moment some distance away reading a magazine under a hair dryer at her favorite beauty shop).

Arthur Morley had a shovel, and he and Mrs. Morley seemed to be arguing heatedly about something.

Michael stopped his bike at the corner of Mrs. Morley's yard. Queenie fell down and skinned her knees again getting off the handlebars, but she scrambled up without fussing, she was so curious to hear what the Morleys were saying.

The voices carried across the yard, but the two speakers did not see the children by the big elm tree.

"You are *not* going to start digging up this yard, Arthur Morley," Mrs. Morley was declaring in no uncertain terms. She stood with her hands on her hips, her head thrust forward defiantly at her brother-in-law.

"Those stamps have got to be around here somewhere," Mr. Morley replied angrily.

"Well, you have no right to dig up my yard."

"George's will gave me the right."

"It did no such thing!"

By now Mr. Morley actually had the shovel halfway

down into the ground by the flower bed. "George was always puttering around here with those flowers of his—"

"No, you *don't*." Mrs. Morley grabbed at the shovel so quickly Arthur was caught off guard, and she had it in her hand before he could stop her and was running toward the house.

"Atta girl," Michael cheered softly under his breath. Queenie jumped up and down and clapped her hands.

Mr. Morley stood by the flower bed, shaking his fist after Mrs. Morley. She clicked up the steps on her high heels, carrying the shovel, and vanished into the house with a resounding whack of the door behind her.

Michael and Queenie waited in the shelter of the tree. Mr. Morley did not even glance in their direction. After a few moments he stalked out to the street and got into his blue car and drove away.

"Bye-bye," Queenie called after him, and Michael gave her a poke.

"Can't you ever be quiet?" he scolded her.

But Arthur Morley was too far down the street to hear Queenie's thin little voice—or if he had, he would not have thought anyone was calling to him. He drove rapidly, glowering at the street, planning to get his own shovel and come back sometime when Mrs. Morley was out.

When the car was gone, Michael wheeled his bike along the yard and up the walk to Mrs. Morley's front-porch steps. She had been watching to see that Arthur went away, and when she saw Michael and Queenie coming, she sighed to herself. "Oh, dear, what do they want now? I hope their mother isn't sending back that cat."

She opened the front door and peered out at them warily. She did not see any cat tucked away anywhere, and she breathed a little easier. She came out on the porch and looked down at Michael's old bike, with the worn seat and scuffed paint. And she was not surprised to see that Queenie was losing her barrette again and had her stockings down at the heel.

"Hey, Mrs. Morley." Michael came up the stairs eagerly. "I thought of a real good place I bet nobody's looked yet."

Queenie came after, belatedly rubbing at her skinned knees and wishing she had a cookie or something good to eat.

"You have?" Mrs. Morley stared at Michael blankly. "Where?"

"Come on, let's go downstairs to the basement and I'll show you."

"All right." Mrs. Morley let the children into the house and they all went down to the basement together.

Nothing had changed much since the day they had been there the week before. The papers were still in disarray, the furniture pushed every which way. Only one thing was different, and this was the presence of a large heap of sand in the middle of the floor.

"What's *that?*" Michael asked with surprise.

Mrs. Morley made a motion of distress.

"I found an old washtub back in the corner of the basement where we used to keep coal when we had a coal-burning furnace, years ago, and it was full of sand. I thought maybe George might have put the album under the sand. So I poured it out."

"Not there, hmm?" Michael said. But it was a good

thought, anyway. It was in just exactly this kind of silly, unexpected place he thought they would find the stamps. He was glad they hadn't been buried in the sand, though. He wanted to be the one to find them—and get the reward.

"Where did you think of looking?" Mrs. Morley asked.

"I'll show you." Michael beckoned and walked along the basement until he was nearly at the back. Then he looked up over his head and pointed with satisfaction.

Mrs. Morley and Queenie looked up. Above their heads, laid across the open beams of the basement, were several large boards. The beams had been a good storage place for these long, flat boards, left over from some carpentry work years before. Some miscellaneous pieces of pipe had been laid across the beams too, but it was the boards that Michael was interested in.

"I bet you the album is up on those boards," he said to Mrs. Morley triumphantly.

Queenie waited curiously. She wondered if Mrs. Morley was going to think more of Michael's idea than she had thought of Queenie's idea to dig up the bushes where India was scratching.

"Well . . . I guess we need a chair. . . ." Mrs. Morley was willing to try anything.

Michael got one of the folding yard chairs and set it up below the boards. He climbed on and was just able to reach up into the beams.

Queenie and Mrs. Morley waited.

One by one he handed the boards down to them.

When the last board had come down and no stamp album seemed to have been hidden among them, Michael still would not give up. He felt around with his hands along the beams. He stretched and stretched to reach as far as he could. His face grew red with exertion.

But at last even he was forced to admit that wherever the stamps were, they were not hidden in the beams by those boards.

"I sometimes wonder if I will *ever* find them," Mrs. Morley moaned, as she began to hand the boards up one by one for Michael to replace.

Queenie wished she had brought India. India knew where those stamps were. They ought to give her a stamp to look at and say, "Now where are the others?" and India would run to the hiding place and show them.

"Maybe somebody else has already found them somehow," Mrs. Morley said sadly. "It says in the will whoever finds them can keep them. Yesterday there was a man down here to read the electric meter—and then the television repairman was here one day last week. Oh, I just don't know."

They all went back upstairs and stood on the porch.

"Come back if you think of any other unusual place," Mrs. Morley said at last. It was growing cold, and she thought she ought to get back in her house.

Michael and Queenie went down the stairs to where the bike lay against the walk at the bottom. Mrs. Morley watched with some trepidation as Queenie climbed onto the handlebars.

"Are you sure that's safe?" Mrs. Morley asked doubtfully. "That bike doesn't look very strong."

It was the most dilapidated bike Mrs. Morley had ever seen.

"Sure it's safe," Michael assured her, and pedaled off with Queenie clutching on with one hand and trying to wave good-bye to Mrs. Morley with the other.

Mrs. Morley was sure they would never make it home, but she had problems of her own to worry about.

She saw them reach the end of the block and round the corner, with Queenie still in place on the handlebars, and she guessed that was as much as she could be expected to do.

Anyway, they had not brought back the cat.

# Thirteen:
## *Discovery*

Michael was sure he could think of some more places around Mrs. Morley's house where the stamp album might be hidden. Walking to and from school the next few days, he tried to think where he would hide something like that if he had it. Sometimes he even thought about this *at* school, and he would be yanked back to arithmetic or spelling words by the sound of the teacher's voice.

"Michael, you're daydreaming."

Then all the kids would turn around and look at him. The girls would giggle and the boys would shoot spitballs at him when the teacher turned her back.

Never mind, Michael would think to himself. When he found the stamps and collected a big reward, he'd show them all.

Every day Michael and Queenie walked home from school a couple of blocks out of their way so that they could go by Mrs. Morley's house. They were curious about Mr. Arthur Morley and the flower bed. They were sure some afternoon they would come walking by and he would be in the yard digging, or he and Mrs. Morley would perhaps be having another argument, snatching a shovel back and forth between them. Either sight, they thought, would be worth seeing.

The first two afternoons they were disappointed. They did not see Mr. Morley's car parked in front of the house, nor any car at all. The house looked very quiet. There was no sign of Mrs. Morley.

The second day the yellow car belonging to Mrs. Morley's daughter was parked at the curb. But there was no one in the yard digging up anything, nor did the flower bed seem to be at all disturbed. The same covering of fallen leaves lay upon the grass, and it was plain that nobody had been digging up anything in the yard.

But on the third day they were rewarded for walking out of their way. Arthur Morley was in the yard. He had a short-handled shovel and he was digging up the flower bed. Mrs. Morley was nowhere in sight.

Now that it was really happening, Michael and Queenie were not sure what to do. They lingered by the fence watching, hoping that Mr. Morley would not find the stamps, and yet wondering if they could be there, in that perfect hiding place under the dead summer flowers.

They did not say a word to each other, but stood at the corner of the yard, Queenie's stomach pressed against the trunk of a tree, her eyes fastened like magnets upon the shoveling man. Michael dug his hands in his trouser pockets. Every blow of the shovel into the ground was a blow struck against his own chances of finding the stamps and collecting a reward.

It was not long before Mr. Morley glanced up and saw them. Although the afternoon was cool, his forehead was perspiring from the unaccustomed physical effort of digging up the heavy autumn earth, and the sight of the two children, so still and intent, angered him. He lifted the shovel and flourished it at them.

"What are you two staring at? Get along there," he called to them.

Queenie took off like a frightened rabbit, but Michael swaggered away with his best show of nonchalance, so that Mr. Morley would see he had not frightened Michael, no sir.

At the corner he caught up with Queenie, who had fallen down and skinned her knees again. Also she had begun to hiccup. Michael helped her up and tried to brush off her knees, but she kept wailing, "Oh, you're hurting me." So he finally gave up, and they walked home with a sense of discouragement to see if there were any popsicles available for Queenie's hiccups.

Not only were there no popsicles available, their mother was not even home.

She had left a note on the kitchen table saying she had taken the baby and gone to visit a neighbor a few blocks away. Queenie got an ice cube and sucked on that, and India came and meowed at the refrigerator door.

"Nice kitty, nice kitty, come and have some supper," Queenie said, as the cuckoo in the kitchen clock popped out to announce four o'clock.

India followed Queenie to the cabinet under the sink where Mrs. Allen had put the carton of cat food Mrs. Morley had given them.

Queenie had been feeding India so much cat food that the first layer of cans was gone, and she began on the second layer. She had thought there would be a third layer underneath, for the box was deep enough for three or four, but when she lifted out a can from the second layer she was surprised to see that there was no shiny metal of cans underneath.

*Instead there was the dark, leather-bound edge of a stamp album.*

Queenie took out a few more cans—and then, working faster and faster in her excitement, she snatched out all of the cans from that second layer.

And lifted out the stamp album.

"Michael! Michael!" Queenie flew out of the kitchen, stumbling over the cans of cat food she had scattered on the floor. Michael was in his bedroom, lying across his bed on his stomach and fixing a model airplane that had lost a wing.

"Michael! Michael!"

Her hair was flying—and she almost dropped the heavy album in her rush.

"Look . . . look . . . look—I found it, I found it. . . ."

Michael looked over his shoulder at the sound of her frantic cries, and she dumped herself, album and all, on the bed beside him.

"The *stamps!*" He lunged up, brushing the airplane aside as he grasped the corners of the heavy book. A great smile spread over his face.

"It was under the cans. . . ." Queenie explained breathlessly, before Michael even had a chance to ask where she had found the album.

Michael couldn't believe his eyes. They lifted the cover, which was lettered in gold "Stamp Album," and saw the name George Morley written across the first page. They began to leaf through the book, although there were so many pages they did not try to look at all of them. Each page was heavy with stamps. Brilliant colors, all sizes.

"Good grief!" Michael said, almost reverently. After all, he was looking at twenty-five thousand dollars!

"What will we do with it?" Queenie wanted to know. There was no one to ask but Michael, and she looked up at him trustfully. She was sure he would know what to do.

"Well . . . we could keep it, maybe," he answered slowly. "It said in the will whoever finds it can keep it. But I don't suppose we could really do that."

"No," said Queenie obediently, "I don't suppose."

They looked at the pages falling one by one as Michael turned them carefully. Twenty-five thousand dollars.

"Look," Michael said, "stamps from countries all over the world. Here's one from Africa."

Queenie bent her head over the book to see the stamp from Africa.

"And here's one from Brazil, South America."

"Couldn't we keep a little of it?" Queenie asked. She shook the hair out of her eyes and stared across the book at Michael.

Michael smiled at her regretfully. "No, I don't think so. It really belongs to Mrs. Morley."

Queenie sighed.

"Come on." Michael closed the album. "Let's go show it to Mrs. Poldini. Think how surprised she'll be."

They raced downstairs, but to their disappointment Mrs. Poldini did not seem to be in. There was no answer as they rang her bell again and again. Whether she was merely out shopping for her supper or was at The Red Moon Tea Shop they did not know.

"Oh, phooey," Queenie wailed.

"Come on," Michael said. "We can't stand here all day. Let's take it to Mrs. Morley. Think how surprised *she'll* be."

Queenie's spirits were restored to think how surprised

—and happy—Mrs. Morley would be when she saw that big fat twenty-five-thousand-dollar stamp album.

They raced upstairs again to get their coats, and Queenie tried to tug up her stockings at the heel so she would look neat.

As they started out again, Michael stopped.

"We can't just go carrying it bare like this," he said. "Maybe we can find a bag or something."

They went into the kitchen, where the cans of cat food still littered the floor. But they did not stop to bother with those. The clock above the stove said nearly four thirty. Soon it would be getting dark.

They opened the cupboard where Mrs. Allen kept empty paper bags from the grocery store, and after discarding a few small ones that were on top, Michael found a large bag that the album would fit into.

India came out from behind the stove and stood watching with her glittering green eyes as they put the album carefully into the bag and Michael folded over the top of the bag so that nobody could see what was inside.

"Oh, thank you, India," Queenie said, blowing a kiss to the cat.

"What are you thanking her for?" Michael asked. But he didn't wait for an answer. "Come on—hurry up and button your coat, Queenie."

They clattered back down the stairs so loudly a lady opened her apartment door and called after them,

"Hey, you kids, where's the fire?"

Panting for breath they reached the street and set off at once for Mrs. Morley's.

"Do you think we'll get a reward?" Queenie asked.

"Maybe this time we will," Michael answered. Boy, if anything deserved a reward, this did.

## Fourteen:

# *Chased*

Queenie chattered all the way to Mrs. Morley's house. "Do you think Mrs. Morley will be surprised?"

"You know it," Michael said. "I bet she never dreamed in a million years she was giving us the album when she gave us the cat food!"

"Do you think that mean old Mr. Morley will be mad?"

"He'll be jumping all over like crazy, he'll be so mad," Michael said with authority. "He'll be the maddest man in the whole town."

Queenie was almost jumping up and down with excitement herself as she thought about this. She trotted along eagerly, trying to keep up with Michael.

As they drew near Mrs. Morley's house, they saw with some dismay that Mr. Arthur Morley was still there in the yard with his shovel.

"Oh-oh," Michael said. "That guy never gives up!" He slowed his walk and tried to decide what to do now.

"What will we do?" Queenie tugged at his sleeve.

"Be quiet, can't you," Michael said nervously. "Let a guy think."

What he thought of that might help a little was to give

Queenie the paper bag to carry. Somehow he thought it would look more innocent if Queenie were carrying it. Girls were always lugging stuff around, dolls and books and stuff like that.

"Here, you hold it until we get in the house," he said. He thrust the paper bag into her arms none too soon, for just then Mr. Morley lifted his head and saw them.

His expression was one of deep vexation. He had been so sure the album was buried in the flower bed, but he had dug nearly all of it, fairly deep down too, and there was nothing to be seen but clumps of roots and dirt.

He watched grimly as Michael and Queenie came along slowly, past the yard, and then turned up the walk to the house. He leaned on his shovel and wiped his forehead with the back of his hand.

"She isn't home," he called to them rudely. "What do you kids want now?"

Queenie cowered behind Michael. Michael stood undecidedly in the middle of the walk.

Mr. Morley was starting to walk toward them.

Michael thought it was time to take off and run as fast as they could—in one direction or the other. Either make a dash the rest of the way to the house, or head for home.

But if Mrs. Morley was away, they couldn't get into the house.

The only reasonable thing to do was run for home and come back again when Mr. Morley was gone.

Michael began to back away slowly, but he still kept his eyes on Mr. Morley and his shovel.

"What do you kids want? I asked you," Mr. Morley repeated, considerably closer now.

"I don't think Mrs. Morley'd like you digging up her yard," Michael said defensively.

"Oh, you don't think so. Well, isn't that too bad."

Mr. Morley kept coming. He was beginning to look madder and madder.

"What've you got in that bag, eh?"

"Run, Queenie!" Michael shouted. And the two flew off together, short-cutting across the grass.

Queenie was clutching the paper bag by the top, instead of holding it in her arms as Michael had held it, and as she ran the heavy album was too much for the thin paper of the bag—the bag began to rip before she realized what was happening, and before their horrified eyes the rip went down the side of the bag with a screeching tearing sound and the album flew out on the grass with a smacking thud.

Mr. Morley uttered a cry of rage and began to come after them at a full run.

Michael swooped down and rescued the album and then caught Queenie's hand and dragged her along up the street after him, she and the shreds of the grocery bag to which she was still clinging for dear life. Queenie couldn't keep anything in anything, Michael thought as he raced blindly over the pavement—anything in anything, cats in hat boxes or stamp albums in paper bags. He just hoped she wouldn't fall down now and ruin everything.

Miraculously, Queenie did not fall. Her feet hardly touched the ground, Michael was dragging her along so fast; her hair was streaming, her paper bag flapping behind her—but she did not fall down.

Around the corner they raced and turned automatically in the direction of their house. Behind them Mr. Morley was running as fast as he could but not gaining on them much.

Halfway along the block Michael looked back, hoping that Mr. Morley had given up. But he was still there. Without his shovel, but running along after them with a fierce look on his face.

At the next corner Michael almost turned the way that would take them home, and then just in time he realized what a mistake this would be. Mr. Morley knew what building they lived in. It would be better not to go that way at all.

Queenie was struggling for breath. Her eyes were beginning to bulge with the effort to run and breathe and not fall down all at the same time.

"Wait . . . wait . . ." she gasped at Michael, but he pulled her along as fast as ever, down into an alley, where he thought they might find some hiding place before they got too out of breath to run anymore. The stamp album, never light at best, felt as if it weighed a ton now. And he could hold it with only one arm, since he had to hold on to Queenie, too.

The alley stretched before them in the gathering shadows of the falling darkness. They had not run far into it when Queenie lost her hold on the paper bag and it blew off like a released balloon. Then, like a stroke of good fortune, they saw a door standing open. Michael bolted in, dragging Queenie after him, and tried to close the door. But it was broken and swung open again, and there was no bolt or lock to hold it from the inside.

Michael didn't stop to fool with the door any longer; he seized Queenie's hand again and began to pull her along through the rooms.

They were in what had been the back room of a store now out of business. A few empty cartons cluttered the floor, enough to get in their way as they hurried through. They tried a door at one end of the room, but it wouldn't open, and then Michael saw another door. This door opened, and they dashed through without a backward look and closed the door behind them.

But there was no lock for it!

Michael could hear Mr. Morley close behind them, heard him kicking aside the empty boxes on the floor of the room they had just come through.

He was still there, still coming after them!

# Fifteen

# Trapped

There was no time to run farther, or anywhere farther to run. They were in the main salesroom of what had been a clothing store. It was nearly dark, for the front windows were covered with boards. Around them stood the empty counters that had once been piled high with men's shirts and pajamas, empty racks where suits and coats had once hung. A mouse disturbed by their arrival scampered across the floor almost at their feet, and Queenie, gasping for breath, had no breath even to cry out in fright when she saw the mouse. Her already wide and startled eyes widened more, but before she had time to be afraid of the mouse Michael had pushed her down behind one of the counters. It was hollow underneath, and he pushed her under and crouched in close beside her.

Michael could feel his own heart pounding against the stamp album as he heard the second door opening behind them.

There was the noise of the door opening.

And then there was silence.

Arthur Morley stood staring around at the large, deserted salesroom. There were a hundred hiding places

here, he could see that at once, and he stood very silently, hoping that by some noise or other the two children would give away where they were.

Queenie was squashed down on the floor under the
counter, with Michael so close against her she could not
move if she had wanted to. Then she felt Michael's hand
come up and cover her mouth, so she knew she must
lie quietly and not make a sound.

"Don't hiccup, Queenie—please don't hiccup," Michael
was praying to himself. Right now that seemed the most
important thing in the world.

Mr. Morley continued to stand in the door, panting
from running, beads of perspiration on his forehead. There
was not a sound, not even from the mouse.

The minutes seemed to drag by forever. Michael had
a pain in his arm from twisting it so he could put his
hand over Queenie's mouth; and one foot was caught
under him in an uncomfortable position. But he did not
dare move.

Whenever he felt Queenie begin to stir, to shift into
some less cramped position, he tightened his hand over
her mouth.

Outside a car went by with a loudspeaker, inviting
everybody to visit the grand opening of Selby's Service
Station.

*"Free balloons for the kiddies, glassware for Mother,"*
the loudspeaker blared.

And then there was music, and voices singing:

> *"Come to Selby's Selby's Selby's,*
> *Come to Selby's for the best."*

*"Grand opening—free balloons for the kiddies, glassware for Mother . . ."* The sound began to fade into the distance.

> *"Come to Selby's Selby's Selby's,*
> *Come to Selby's for the best. . . ."*

Mr. Morley began to walk cautiously into the room. He did not even close the door behind him, and he walked on his tiptoes. But even with these precautions Michael could hear the faint squeak of an old floorboard now and then. When he thought he dared, Michael moved just enough to see around the corner of the counter— and saw that Mr. Morley was standing right in front of *their* counter. Michael was staring at the back of his leg and one brown shoe, dusty from the earth of the flower bed.

After what seemed to Michael a long, long time, the leg and shoe moved on. Michael waited, and a floorboard squeaked somewhere farther across the room. It seemed their only chance, for if they stayed, sooner or later Mr. Morley would look behind every counter.

Michael grabbed Queenie's hand again and broke for the open door.

They never even stopped to look behind, but shot through the door, through the storeroom, and out into the alley again.

Mr. Morley was after them at once. Through the back room of the store and out into the alley. He could catch up with them easily enough now, he thought, the little monsters!

Then suddenly a yellow cat sprang from behind a gar-

bage can in the alley, right under Mr. Morley's feet.
Mr. Morley stumbled and fell, his feet tangling with the
flashing yellow body. The cat let out a dreadful screech
and sprang up on the garbage can. The children vanished
around the corner of the alley, and Mr. Morley looked
up belligerently into the green eyes of India, the dead
man's cat, standing on the garbage can, back arched, tail
lashing. And he thought the little mouth parted and the
pointed cat teeth showed in a malicious grin.

Arthur Morley picked himself up and brushed off his
trousers.

The children were out of sight.

There was nobody but India, and before starting back
to Mrs. Morley's house Arthur Morley picked up a tin can
lying in the alley and hurled it at the cat. But it missed.

## Sixteen:

# All Is Revealed

"All is revealed," Mrs. Poldini said.

She was sitting grandly on one of her green chairs, hands folded complacently in her lap. Lamplight brightened the shabby room, the empty bird cage, and George Morley's photograph on the piano. In the kitchen the teakettle hissed softly.

Mrs. Morley sat on the edge of her chair—for she still did not think the chairs looked very clean—and Michael and Queenie sat together on the piano bench. Mrs. Morley held the stamp album on her lap and occasionally ran her fingers over the cover to assure herself that it was really in her possession, that it would not disappear in this strange, steamy room.

"I tell you, look in your heart," Mrs. Poldini said.

When the old woman spoke, Mrs. Morley looked up with a startled expression.

*"You* told me?" she said. "I thought that was a message from my dead husband."

Mrs. Poldini shuddered inwardly. Her eyelids closed wearily over her great dark mysterious eyes.

"I tell you what husband say," she answered slowly and carefully. "Look in your heart."

She opened her eyes and gazed meditatively at Mrs. Morley, who fluttered one hand vaguely.

"Your husband want someone to love cat," Mrs. Poldini continued in her deep and somber voice. "He thinks whoever is kind in their heart to do this, find stamps."

"But what if the stamps had just been thrown out by mistake, hidden that ridiculous way?" Mrs. Morley muttered.

"Your husband think that serve everybody right." Mrs. Poldini shrugged. "Nobody love cat, nobody get stamps."

Mrs. Morley straightened herself and opened her mouth to protest, but Mrs. Poldini silenced her with a motion.

"Children love cat. Maybe stamps theirs now."

The expression on Mrs. Morley's face said she would certainly hope *not*. That will was merely a technicality. Whoever found the stamps indeed! The stamps were rightfully *hers*.

"Gee, we wouldn't keep them, Mrs. Morley," Michael exclaimed.

"The stamps are rightfully mine," Mrs. Morley said as calmly as she could.

"I think so." Mrs. Poldini nodded heavily.

But we would like a reward, Michael thought to himself. He sat very still on the piano bench.

Queenie smiled guilelessly at Mrs. Morley.

"I knew India would help us," she said.

In her lap the ugly yellow cat opened its eyes and squinted at the lamplight.

"I don't think I have to share them with Arthur, either," Mrs. Morley continued. She wanted everything set straight, so there would be no doubts on anybody's part.

Mrs. Poldini nodded absently.

"For that, too, you look in your heart."

Mrs. Morley felt that her heart told her to keep all the money she would get from the sale of the album. Greedy old Arthur and that silly Letitia had already torn up half the house and ruined the flower bed. Mrs. Morley's heart told her she could use a new rug for her living room and a new set of dishes. The rest would go nicely into her savings account for her old age.

But the children . . . Mrs. Morley's gaze shifted to them thoughtfully. True, they might have legally claimed the stamps as theirs, according to the terms of George's foolish will. But they hadn't. And they had tried to help her all along. . . . For the boy, a new bike perhaps; and for the girl? Mrs. Morley smiled faintly in spite of herself. Oh, to see that skinned-kneed, scraggly little thing in a pretty ruffly pink dress, with a pair of shiny patent leather party shoes like Dorothea used to love so much when she was Queenie's age. Mrs. Morley's heart told her that this much surely she could spare.

Queenie stirred restlessly. It had been an exciting afternoon, finding the stamps and being chased by Mr. Morley. Then, when they had reached home safely, Mrs. Poldini had been back from her shopping, her bag loaded with cabbage and tea and the big soft cinnamon rolls she ate for her breakfast. Mrs. Poldini had called Mrs. Morley on the telephone, and Queenie and Michael had run upstairs to their own apartment just long enough to tell their mother they had found some missing stamps for a lady Mrs. Poldini knew and they wanted to be at Mrs. Poldini's when she came.

"All right then, but don't spoil your suppers with that awful stuff she cooks," Mrs. Allen had warned.

Yes, it had been an exciting afternoon. Now Queenie wanted to go into the bedroom and try on some of Mrs. Poldini's shoes.

Her eyes sought Mrs. Poldini's, and at a nod from her, Queenie released India, slipped from the piano bench and went into the bedroom—a room of unending delights for her with its clutter of circus clothes and the forty pairs of shoes.

When she came tottering out a few minutes later, wearing a pair of red shoes with tall thin heels (which Mrs. Poldini had owned for twenty years or more), Michael was teasing India with a piece of fringe from the piano-bench cover and Mrs. Morley sat beside Mrs. Poldini at the purple-covered table, drinking a cup of tea and considering her heart, which spoke to her ever more certainly about a shiny new bike and a pink dress and party shoes.

George Morley's photograph smiled down from the piano, and from the kitchen came the aroma of Mrs. Poldini's cabbage cooking for supper.